G R JORDAN

The Nationalist Express

A Kirsten Stewart Thriller #4

"The fascination of hunting as a sport
depends almost wholly on whether
you are at the right or the wrong end
of the gun."

P.G. Wodehouse

Contents

Acknowledgement

To Susan, Jean and Rosemary for your work in bringing this novel to completion, your time and effort is deeply appreciated.

Novels by G R Jordan

The Highlands and Islands Detective series (Crime)

1. Water's Edge
2. The Bothy
3. The Horror Weekend
4. The Small Ferry
5. Dead at Third Man
6. The Pirate Club
7. A Personal Agenda
8. A Just Punishment
9. The Numerous Deaths of Santa Claus
10. Our Gated Community
11. The Satchel
12. Culhwch Alpha
13. Fair Market Value
14. The Coach Bomber
15. The Culling at Singing Sands
16. Where Justice Fails
17. The Cortado Club
18. Cleared to Die

Kirsten Stewart Thrillers (Thriller)

1. A Shot at Democracy
2. The Hunted Child
3. The Express Wishes of Mr MacIver
4. The Nationalist Express
5. The Hunt for 'Red' Anna

The Contessa Munroe Mysteries (Cozy Mystery)

1. Corpse Reviver
2. Frostbite
3. Cobra's Fang

The Patrick Smythe Series (Crime)

1. The Disappearance of Russell Hadleigh
2. The Graves of Calgary Bay
3. The Fairy Pools Gathering

Austerley & Kirkgordon Series (Fantasy)

1. Crescendo!
2. The Darkness at Dillingham
3. Dagon's Revenge
4. Ship of Doom

Supernatural and Elder Threat Assessment Agency (SETAA) Series (Fantasy)

1. Scarlett O'Meara: Beastmaster

Island Adventures Series (Cosy Fantasy Adventure)

1. Surface Tensions

Dark Wen Series (Horror Fantasy)

1. The Blasphemous Welcome
2. The Demon's Chalice

Chapter 01

The morning was cool, one of those February mornings with dew on the grass and a chill in the air. The sun was slowly fighting back, albeit it was low in the blue sky. Before Kirsten was parkland that rolled in green with just a few early morning dog walkers about, and directly in front of her was a steaming cup of black coffee. She was hoping she wasn't too bleary-eyed, trusting that she seemed pleased to be there.

Kirsten was happy to be here, but the fatigue from the previous night was probably showing. She had caught the late flight down from Inverness but had been delayed and she hadn't arrived in London until two in the morning. By the time she'd found a hotel and finally got into bed, it was half-past three. She had crazily said they should meet for breakfast, said they should be up before everyone else to take in the quiet of the day. Kirsten had grabbed the train towards the park on the edge of the city and had proceeded to the coffee house he had described. Within all the hustle and bustle, the place was an oasis, but she lived up in the highlands and a view like this was almost commonplace.

She fought back the chill she felt, dressed in her jeans and

T-shirt, with a simple hoodie over the top. She thought about a hairband and tying her hair up but instead, she brushed it as best she could, letting it hang out loose. It had been a long while since Kirsten had gone to meet a man that she was particularly interested in, but strangely enough, this one was so far away from her. She had met him when called down to London on business previously.

Life in the Secret Services wasn't easy. Often you met people that you needed to forget, or you couldn't approach in anything but a purely work basis. Bringing in others from outside work would put them at risk, and so Kirsten had been surprised that something inside her had fallen for the man who had been her first driver here in London. She'd come down a couple of times since, merely to chat, the pair of them taking refuge in someone they could talk to for a while. Able to mention work without delving too deep into exactly what each other had done, they were able to sympathise with the more brutal aspects of their jobs.

But this meeting was initiated by Kirsten. She had cleared a week away from the office, a week of being able to spend time with a man she saw so rarely. She was nervous. Would he be all she wanted him to be? All she had seen so far was good; quick meetings were easy. Flitting in here and there—but to have a sustained week would be something different.

Kirsten scanned the horizon, looking for any signs of the arrival of her man, but she only saw a dog walker, a young man maybe twenty, jogging along with a decidedly small dog behind him. The legs of the animal didn't seem long enough to accommodate the pace that the man was trying to set, and Kirsten could see the lead being pulled time and time again. The dog snapped into a sudden scurry. *That wasn't right*, she thought. *He can't do that to an animal.* Her mind quickly glossed over it, and she looked the other way, finally seeing her man in the distance.

Kirsten had gone for the casual look. The jeans, the hoodie, trying to take away from work. Usually, when the two of them met on business, he was dressed smartly, and she would sit in the back of the car to be taken to meet those higher up in the organisation. Kirsten would be wearing a skirt, a blouse, maybe a jacket. Always looking the part as Anna Hunt, her boss, would put it. Back in her own office in Inverness, Kirsten was rarely ever seen in a skirt. She didn't like them.

She'd been brought up in a mixed martial arts ring, learning to fight from an early age where they didn't parade around in suits. Nowadays that had all changed, but there weren't that many in the ring. Of course, in the service, it used to be all men in the important jobs, so suits went down well. These days, there was more equality, though within the service, you still had to look the part. Kirsten got the job done and she did it well. Her old boss Macleod had never asked for any of this. He was just happy with the work she did.

Scotland was in turmoil, and Kirsten was glad to be away from it. As she watched her man approach, she thought back to the recent weeks. The great debate was on again. Should Scotland be part of the United Kingdom? Should it break away to be an independent country? There were plenty of rallies, plenty of shouting of this and that. Politicians consistently on the TV, the polls telling you one thing or another. Kirsten was not a person to worry too much about politics.

Anna Hunt had said this was a flaw and she needed to gain a deeper understanding of the subject, but Anna had never said Kirsten needed to take a political side. After all, Kirsten could be working for any government that the public voted in. She preferred to see herself as someone who defended the country, not any faction. She had saved the First Minister's life, but not because she was SNP, or Labour, or Tory—simply because it was someone in need of saving. Kirsten was embarrassed to say it out loud, but she'd saved democracy, when to preserve it was deep within her grasp. Although to Kirsten, it was someone who was the target of a killer and she needed to stop them. That was the way she saw it when she was on Macleod's murder team, and that was how she saw it now.

Anna Hunt had been reluctant at first to let Kirsten come away at such a time of national change. The team had been working hard, looking around for any inkling that there could be terrorist activity, any sort of dark agendas in the run-up to such a momentous occasion, but they found nothing. Not even a whisper, and so Kirsten had managed to take a week off with Anna's consent, if not her blessing.

Kirsten looked again and saw her man approaching. He was wearing a suit. *Damn it*, thought Kirsten. *Damn, damn, damn. I don't need this. This was my week. This was our time, chance to get to know him.* She could see he was shuffling along, not using his usual stride. Maybe he was avoiding the moment, but he needn't have done, as Kirsten knew what was coming. As he approached, Kirsten smiled and tried to take the severely cheesed-off look from her face.

'Sorry,' he said. 'Anna Hunt would like you to contact her and then you're on the plane to Scotland.'

'Don't I get a hello? Nice to see you? I mean, if I'd known, I would have invited you around to the hotel last night.'

The man's face seemed to pick up. 'And if I'd have known, I'd have been there,' he said. 'Anna's awaiting the call, sorry.'

'Go get a coffee and bring it back,' said Kirsten. 'I can't get on the commercial flight?' The man shook his head. 'Good, now wait for me. Go get a coffee.'

Kirsten watched him make his way inside the building behind her to order a coffee and she kept her eyes on him until he disappeared from view. He did work a suit well. The lines were crisp, the charcoal colour seemed to suit him, and his shoulders held the jacket well.

Kirsten took out her phone, dialled the number for Anna Hunt, and sat back, holding the device to her ear. She wanted to swear at the woman. She wanted to rage at her. *What sort of an industry was this who didn't get proper holidays? What sort of an industry was this?* thought Kirsten. *Even Macleod gave you holidays. Well, that wasn't true, was it? If something big was happening, you were in for it.*

'Anna Hunt.'

'Did you plan to ruin my weekend or was it just something that you threw together this morning?'

'Sorry about that,' said Anna. 'I am actually sorry, but I need you to get back up north. I think you're going to need to talk to your old boss. We've had word Angus Macritchie's dead.'

'Macritchie, the independent?'

'I see your political knowledge is improving. Yes, Mr. Macritchie was found dead, we believe, in the early hours of the morning. As you know, although he was an independent candidate, and had managed to be an MSP in the Inverness area for quite for some time, he was a strong advocate for the union. This close to the referendum means we need to make sure this is not a concerted effort.'

'Do we know how he died?'

'No, not exactly,' said Anna. 'I know they've put Macleod's

murder team on to it, so I need you back up there to assess and also put him in check if we need to. See if we need to run this.'

'So, you're basically not just taking me away from my holiday, you want me to go and piss off my old boss and friend?'

'Well, you took the job,' said Anna. 'You could have stayed with him. The plane's ready for you. I suggest you get a move on.'

'Have you told Dom or Carrie Anne yet?'

'No, but they'll be waking up to it. I suggest you get on the phone to them to say what you want to do. I thought it best if you go out, speak to Macleod. From what I gathered, he's not a man to be easily swayed. He might appreciate the services we carry out, but I doubt that will stop him investigating and we might have to do that.'

'No, he won't take it well,' said Kirsten. 'I'll get Dom and Carrie Anne on some fishing work, see if they can find out what was going around the politician and I'll get Justin to get plenty of the background, but you're right. It's probably best that I go and cover off. It does seem strange though. For all we've done, Anna, and we have covered the territory over the last lot of weeks, there hasn't been a sniff of anything.'

'That's not good,' said Anna. 'The trouble when you don't get a sniff of anything is it's usually well hidden. When there's rumblings, background noise, that's fine, but when everything's shut up, that means something's happening.'

Kirsten tried to get her head around the perverse logic, but Anna was right. Kirsten trusted her, for the woman had the experience.

'I'll get off the phone now,' said Anna.

'Best do,' said Kirsten, 'and I best get off to the plane.'

'I take it you told him to go and get a coffee?' Kirsten went silent on the phone. 'It's all right,' said Anna, 'if I'd travelled all the way down to meet someone I was keen on, I'd want at least one coffee with him. Just don't hang about and don't bring him back up the road with you either. It's tempting, but trust me, he'll get in the way.'

'I wasn't thinking of bringing him back up the road.' said Kirsten, her voice full of annoyance, but her mind shocked at how Anna had guessed the thought that had gone through her head. 'I'll speak to you as soon as I've got something,' continued Kirsten.

She put the phone away and started sipping her coffee until a suited man slipped into the seat in front of her. She looked at his coffee inside a paper cup and not one of the branded mugs that Kirsten was drinking from.

'You didn't have to do that.'

'Well, I thought you'd be running for the airport,' he said. 'I know you have to go.'

'I don't have to go yet,' said Kirsten. 'I maybe have to go in twenty minutes.' The pair laughed out loud.

'Is this what is to be?' asked the man. 'We plan something; it all goes wrong. Maybe I should move up the road.'

Kirsten's heart jumped. *That was an idea*, she thought, but she didn't want to look too pushy. 'Let's just do a reset on it,' she said. 'Let's try and do this again once I get clear up north.'

'I think it has to do with the referendum.'

'Everything's to do with the referendum at the moment up north.' said Kirsten, shaking her head. 'I don't want to talk about that for twenty minutes. Hey, how are you? You look well. You look damn well.' She reached forward with her hand, he reciprocated, and they moved closer so they were on the same side of the table.

'I feel like a little kid,' said Kirsten. 'Do you know that? I was down here trying to be all cool and calm.'

'I could tell,' he said. 'You've got your jeans. You've got your hoodie. It's very you, but your hair's not even brushed.'

Kirsten laughed. 'Is this what it is like to get away with nothing? The joy of dating an operative,' she said quietly.

'It's okay. It means I can appreciate you better,' he said and laughed.

'Twenty minutes,' said Kirsten. 'Tell me something about you I don't know.' She let herself relax a little, a half eye on her watch and listened to the man talk. She'd be back down soon enough. Oh, she'd definitely be back.

Chapter 02

Kirsten stared at the Moray Firth as the business jet rolled into Inverness Airport. She hadn't bothered to change, still in her jeans and hoodie, and her hair was still not tied up. This was back to business. With how cold it was, she put a beanie hat on as well.

On the flight, she had contacted Dom, her second at the Inverness base, but he was already on to what she wanted him to do. He was running background checks on the politician, calling in favours to find out his movements and sending Carrie Anne out to check up on any contacts made. Kirsten appreciated the thoroughness of her team, and she knew Dom, the experienced field agent, and Carrie Anne, part field agent, part analyst, would get their teeth stuck into the problems.

Her other colleague at the base, Justin Chivers, would be pulling records, bank accounts, and anything else he could find on the politician. Some of it, the police would struggle to get hold of, and certainly not as quickly as Justin could. The man was a whizz on the computers and had been an experienced operative for Anna Hunt. A man whom Kirsten was now delighted to have, a gift from her boss.

The sun was shining but the air was cold as Kirsten stepped into a car and was driven back to her base. She found everyone, except Justin, out, and after briefly dropping her luggage off, she jumped into her own car and drove to the politician's house where the poor man had been found dead. Angus Macritchie, although being an MSP for the area north of Inverness, lived quite far up, all the way to Dornoch, and Kirsten made her way as quickly as she could, enjoying the surroundings.

As she got to the small housing estate, she noticed the quality of the houses within it. It may have been built forty years ago, but when they built these houses, they were all five- or six-bedroom affairs. Grand pillars at the front door of a house that nowadays would have set you back several hundred thousand, if not closer to half a million.

Angus Macritchie was a well-loved politician, someone who stood for the area. He was constantly on the television, giving his views and, in the recent debates, had been a strong advocate for the Union, stating that Scotland needed the other three countries with it to keep it safe and strong. He had argued about where money wasn't going to come from when Scotland went independent and even got involved in several heated debates on television.

For those trying to back the unionist standpoint, the fact that an independent politician of his calibre was promoting their cause was a boon. For those looking for a more nationalistic agenda and to seek independence, it was a bitter blow.

Kirsten pulled the car over when she saw the cordon of police around a small close containing Macritchie's house. She approached the cordon, took out her credentials and showed them to one of the police officers on the line. He nodded, let her through, and she walked up towards the house.

On one side of the house was a forensic van. She recognised it was Jona Nakamura's, the head of forensics at Inverness

Police Station. Looking around, she couldn't find her old boss, Macleod. The detective inspector would be somewhere, but she just wasn't sure where.

She saw a woman with purple hair, older than herself, who was ordering some police constables about. She had a large shawl thrown around her shoulders that looked snug, and she was wearing trousers with boots that went up almost to her knees. There was a broach on the shawl and Kirsten recognised it as something of quality.

'You want something?' the woman in the purple hair asked.

Kirsten strode over and quietly said, 'I'm looking for DI Macleod. Is he here?'

'He's here all right, but he's in the middle of a murder investigation. Who are you?'

Kirsten pulled out her credentials again which showed she was part of the secret services.

'Stewart. Kirsten Stewart,' the woman said, almost chewing the words. 'I thought you'd be taller.'

The one thing Kirsten wasn't, was tall. When she'd worked in the murder team, she was always being dwarfed by her boss, six-feet-tall Hope McGrath, but the red-haired woman wasn't there either.

'And you are?'

'Your replacement, Clarissa Urquhart. I'm sure Seoras is going to be delighted to see you. Wouldn't mind watching this.'

'Is he in that mood?' The woman nearly choked with laughter.

'He's always in the mood,' said Clarissa, chortling to herself. 'Come on. Let's go find him for you.'

Clarissa led the way inside the house before taking Kirsten

through to the back. In the kitchen, Clarissa made sure that Kirsten stayed well to one side of the floor, where the forensic team were working. Looking down, Kirsten could see a body. A man in his sixties, greying hair, but rather distinguished looking. The face was packed, not chubby, like it was struggling to contain whatever it was inside. He'd clearly been wearing his dressing gown when he was killed. There was also a Scottish flag wrapped around him.

Kirsten thought this was the craziest bit of all. *These days, the flag was being used as a call for independence, but Scotland was Scotland, whether it was independent or not.* Whether she stood one side or the other, she would stand and wave that flag, and yet it was being used by some as a counter to the Union flag.

'He's out the back,' said Clarissa. 'I can feel his moodiness from here.' Clarissa strode through the back door into the garden where she stopped short of Macleod and turned to Kirsten. 'I guess I'll let you make your introductions,' said Clarissa.

'I thought you wanted to watch,' said Kirsten.

'He'd just chase me off,' said Clarissa. 'He's not daft either. Good luck.' Clarissa marched off.

Kirsten walked forward and could see Macleod was in that contemplative stance that he often took. Hope McGrath, the sergeant on the murder team, was a woman of action, and although Macleod did his day's work of chasing criminals, he was the brains. He was the one who could think through the issues, think through why someone was killed. She often thought he saw things before he could prove them. He had that hunch, that feeling, and he was rarely wrong.

'Detective Inspector.'

Macleod spun on his heel. Kirsten was shocked at how weary

the man's face looked. 'You could smile,' said Kirsten.

'Good to see you,' said Macleod. 'Well, in a personal sense. In a professional sense, why are you here?'

'See if I need to take this one off you,' said Kirsten. 'Do you want to tell me about it?'

'Have you seen them inside?' said Macleod. 'That's how they found him on his kitchen floor. Wife came down this morning. They broke in quietly. Jona reckons they probably chloroformed the wife or something similar, knocked her out to keep her quiet. Took him down and tortured him. He's got stab marks all the way up his chest. His toenails are missing and then they killed him. Cut his throat and wrapped him up in a St Andrews flag.'

'Any idea who?'

'None,' said Macleod. 'This is out of the blue, completely out of the blue. No indications from anyone that this sort of thing was going to happen. Did you know?'

The tone was almost accusatory. 'No, we didn't,' said Kirsten. 'There's been nothing. That's why I'm here. I'm meant to be on a week's leave.'

'That side never changes, does it? It's never part of what we work for. No one's taken responsibility yet either,' said Macleod. He was standing in a large coat but Kirsten could see he was getting cold.

'Do you want to go inside?'

'No. Let's go see Jona. I think she's out in the wagon. She can tell you what little she knows. As far as I gathered, she's having difficulty finding any evidence that people were here. Well, any evidence other than the fact that the wife was clearly drugged in some funny way and Angus Macritchie was tortured and killed.'

Kirsten followed Macleod as he trudged by the side of the house up to the forensic van. An officer on the door opened it and shouted to Jona that the detective inspector was here.

'Kirsten Stewart,' said Jona, 'Good to see you again. I'm afraid I haven't got much for you. We found one footprint outside. It's quite heavy set. I've done an analysis on it and we think it's a male foot. I reckon the man might be somewhere in the range of six feet tall and he's heavyset. Hopefully, that narrows down your selection of suspects, but I have no DNA; I have nothing. Whoever came in here was good.'

'We're not talking some sort of lunatic? We're not talking some sort of random killing, someone who's just got upset by the debate?' asked Kirsten.

'No,' said Macleod. 'Look at it. Look at the detail. Look at how well they've done this. Tortured and left in a Scottish flag, but with nothing left behind. It's quite a statement.'

'It's a heck of a statement,' said Kirsten. 'Coming up to the referendum as well, but also a strange one.'

'How so?' said Macleod.

'I thought he was independent, Macritchie.'

'He was,' said Jona. 'You're right. Why would you kill the independent? He's swinging to that side. Why wouldn't you kill someone who was out and out unionist, someone who was standing there shouting it from the rooftops from the very beginning?'

'Because this will strike more fear,' said Kirsten. 'If it was just somebody that was off the scale, he would be seen as a mad man. This murder is well considered; somebody who was making the arguments definitely got a stronger effect, more terrifying.'

'Murder is murder,' said Macleod, 'whichever poor man ends

up on the end of it. What's more worrying about this one, even though it's politics, what bothers me is it was so clean, so well done. I don't know if there were professionals involved, but certainly people who are highly trained. We need to look at ex-military. We need to look at people who can do this type of killing. If they're being paid, well, we're deep into it because there's enough money to pay for this to be done again.'

'If they're not being paid, then there'll be more,' said Jona. 'Why would you stop at one?'

'You don't think they're trying to swing public opinion?' asked Kirsten. 'Terrify people into voting to be independent?'

'That doesn't work,' said Macleod. 'You can't terrify people into voting by killing off people. You terrify them into it by saying "you haven't got enough money. The taxes will go up." You terrify them by saying, "Your life is going to change because of X, Y, and Z. Your kids won't get to school." That's where you terrify people. Politicians can get into that. This sort of person, this is hatred. This is somebody that's going to make a statement. This is terror in the sense that you deal with,' said Macleod.

'I'm going to go and have a look around the house if that's all right, Seoras.'

'You think we can't cut it? You'll not find anything Jona hasn't found yet.'

'Another set of eyes won't hurt,' said Kirsten.

'We're professional here, too; you know we can do this. You worked with me long enough.'

'It's okay,' said Kirsten. 'I know, but you trained me. You would run your set of eyes over this if you were here in my place. You'd be the first to check it yourself.'

'Go on then,' said Macleod.

Kirsten left the van to walk around the rather palatial house. She strolled around the rooms, her eyes sweeping across every detail. She felt a little unbalanced, but in her mind what Macleod had said kept ringing. The politicians can terrorise you with tax raises, terrorising school closures but this wasn't that. This was real terror because it came out of hatred.

Chapter 03

Kirsten parked her car and made way to her office in the old town of Inverness. The building looked like it had a shop on the ground floor and was run as a business by personnel who did not know what went on up above but knew the work above needed protecting. Duly, they recognised Kirsten as she came in, giving her a wave and watched her as she disappeared up the stairs. Reaching her own office, Kirsten clumped through the door, flopped down on her chair, and stared out of the window.

Her deliberations were cut as Dominic walked into the room, clutching a piece of paper. Dominic had been hired by Kirsten to be a mainstay of the team as he had been an experienced field agent for many years. He had what Kirsten lacked, experience.

'Been running through recent communications. I think I've got something; it's very low key. A muttering really. A Jennifer Galson, she's one of the leading union-promoting politicians. I think she's Labour. Her name was dropped in a phone conversation that we were listening to six, seven weeks ago. The source tends to be publishing views that are reasonably hardcore. There's nothing saying that they'll kill her, but it's the only politician name we've got out there at the moment.'

Kirsten rolled her shoulders up, arched her back and stretched. It seemed not long ago that she was sitting in a coffee shop on the outskirts of London, waiting for the start of what was going to be a fabulous week. Instead, she got twenty minutes. Twenty minutes of trying to make a connection in a more meaningful way with a man she barely knew.

'Is that your reading of it, Dom?' she asked. 'You say she's mentioned, but there's no idea of assassination, of taking her out, beating her up or anything?'

'Not directly in the communication we saw, but she's the only word out there. Having seen the Macritchie killing, do you think there's going to be another?'

'I don't know,' said Kirsten. 'I really don't know. However, my old boss Macleod seemed to think so. I've learned to trust his nose.'

'Well, on the other hand,' said Dom, 'we haven't really got a lot else to go on. Checked in with Justin. He's going to see you in a while but he hasn't got an awful lot, probably more likely that you're going to have to do an ear to the ground situation, get out and about, see what the word is. Although quite how we'll walk straight into the middle of those conversations I don't know. Do we have any operatives working within the nationalist side of things?'

'There are a few, but we haven't got anything from them. I'm beginning to believe this isn't general fundamentalists. It may be somebody else. Heaven forbid it might even be somebody solo. One thing that does bother me though, Dom, is the fact that these guys were good. They got into a house, managed to drug the wife, torture and kill their victim, and get out while leaving next-to-no clues. There was only one footprint left behind. That was because of a rather random piece of mud on the ground. However, the description we get from it of an approximately six-foot man, well-built, isn't exactly easy to narrow down.'

Dom smiled. 'Well, that's about par for the course, isn't it? But Anna's called you back. She's got to be worried.'

'I think she's more bothered about the fact that this could incite other things. She wants to make sure there's nothing really behind it. Obviously, there's a murder, but Macleod can deal with that. We need to be looking at the picture beyond. Is this stirring up something else?'

'Well, at the moment,' said Dom, 'I can't say.'

'In the meantime, if all we've got is a name, Jennifer Galson, and it's been put out there, I suggest that you and Carrie Anne cover that off. Keep eyes on, see if there's any unusual movement around her. See if anyone's tailing her. That's all we've got to go on. I'll speak to Justin and see what he's got for me, push a lead from there. After a day or two, if nothing's coming up at your end, Dom, we'll bring one of you back at least, head off onto other things.'

Dom nodded and took his leave. Kirsten stood up, walked across her office, and switched on the coffee machine. It was always primed and ready to go, a little trait that Justin had got into. If ever he knew Kirsten was coming in and he knew she would be weary, the coffee was always ready. There was one thing that she had been impressed with, how she connected with him. A guy, who, when she initially started to work with him, she thought of as an outright perv. Now she understood that her kind was not the type of individual he was after.

It was twenty minutes before Justin came through. Kirsten pointed to the coffee machine, whereupon Justin nodded enthusiastically. Together they sat down around Kirsten's desk and Justin put his tablet down in front of him.

'I've been checking through links, trying to see where there's any correspondence going on, even see if there's any money traced to any nationalist organisations. Reports we have from our contacts working out in the field are the Clansmen in Dingwall would be a good place to start. It seems a lot of the people who are into rather extreme nationalism drink in there. It's on a bit of a rough estate.'

'Do you have an address for it?' asked Kirsten.

'Of course, always ready for what the boss wants. It's how you stay ahead in this game after all, isn't it?' said Justin, smiling. He wrote down the address on a piece of paper and passed it across to Kirsten. 'I would be careful though,' he said. 'Apparently, it can get a bit rough in there. Not sure it's a family-friendly pub, or even if it's particularly a woman's pub.'

'You know I can handle myself, don't you?'

'Even so, boss,' said Justin, 'just be careful. Make sure you take your beeper with you.'

Kirsten's beeper was an automatic button she could press if she was in trouble. Although she didn't take it on the more serious missions, when she was generally travelling about, she would have it to hand.

'It's quite touching the way you look after me,' said Kirsten, smiling, 'But I think I better go and do this now. If I leave it until later in the day, I'm going to be too tired. Besides, according to Dom, we've got nothing to go on.' She wandered over to the window of the building, stretching again, fighting the day. 'Do you know I went all the way down there for twenty minutes with him? Twenty minutes was all I got and he was wearing a suit.'

'Suits can be good,' said Justin. 'Some men rock a suit.'

'Do I look like a woman who wants a man in a suit?' She let her hands indicate the hoodie she was wearing, and the jeans.

'Opposites attract,' said Justin, laughing. 'I'll get back onto our sources. I've sent a few out to see if they can find anything else, but in honesty, it just seems so quiet. All the noise seems to be coming from the politicians.'

'You'll be voting in the referendum?' queried Kirsten.

'Of course,' said Justin. 'I live up here now, don't I?'

Justin was originally from England, unlike the other two agents that worked with Kirsten. 'Can't let the union down,' he said. 'Do this one for Her Majesty.' Justin stood up, hand across his chest and held the pose until he saw Kirsten laughing. 'Well, maybe not that much,' he said, 'but I certainly don't want to see Scotland on their own. It's not going to work for me. What about you?'

'I honestly couldn't care less,' said Kirsten. 'I get fed up with all this. People just need to get on. Whether my brother was Scottish or not, look at him. He still ended up in a home, didn't he? Makes no difference to me. Don't mind waving the Scottish flying for the haggis and Loch Ness and sell it all to the tourists but as long as you got what you want, roof over your head, good friends, good family, what on earth else do you want?'

'Very enlightened individual, my boss,' said Justin. 'Just a pity that the rest of the population of the United Kingdom is not so well versed in what it is to be reasonable.'

He walked out of the room laughing and Kirsten nearly threw something after him. The referendum vote was no laughing matter, however. She'd seen on the news where posters had been defaced, people had come to bitter blow of words, although any violence had been minimal, but the country was on a powder keg ready to explode. She wondered what would happen, depending how the result went. Would those with a deeper independence agenda rise up if the vote didn't go their way? Would those in the United Kingdom launch protests? It was just a mess, something that Kirsten couldn't be careless about.

She looked around, grabbed her keys, and made her way down to her car, then thought better of it and caught a bus out to the estate in Dingwall. It took Kirsten about an hour to get there, but she understood what Justin meant when he said it was a rather rough place. The front doors of the pub had glass panes that were boarded over. You could see nothing of the interior from the exterior, but you could tell what sort of a pub it was, the sort of place you might get a few fights on a Saturday night. A place where the locals would stare at you if they didn't like the look of you.

Kirsten pushed the front door open and marched in. The interior was dark, the lighting dim, and the wooden tables and occasional chairs gave a look of easily replaced items. The bar seemed to sell larger and shorts. There was cheap blended whisky, but only one bottle of what she would require, and what many Scottish people would say was genuine whisky, a single malt. However, she wasn't too familiar with the name of it.

Kirsten ordered a double from the bar, told the man to make it neat, and took it over to the corner. Looking around, she saw she was the only woman in the establishment and reckoned that Dom might have been a better bet for gaining information. Regardless, she sat down, took off her hoodie top and placed it beside her. Almost immediately, a man came over, and sat down directly beside her. He was of medium height, which meant he was taller than Kirsten. His face had many cuts on it, like he'd been involved in a few brawls. She could smell the booze off him and he slurred his words when he spoke to her.

'You're looking for some business, love?'

There weren't many places that Kirsten went into that she was instantly thought of as a hooker. Although she was pleased for the cover, she didn't feel that it said much about her as a person.

'I'm just having a drink,' said Kirsten. 'You want to buy me one?'

'If you want to come in my corner, I'll get you one. Do me a favour. It's dark enough, but the other guys might watch a bit.'

Kirsten felt sick to the core, but she shook her head and knocked down some of the whisky. The man spent the next ten minutes talking to her and she generally ignored him, listening instead to a conversation three tables away. There was plenty of talk about the referendum and sending those English packing. Scotland for the Scots, talk of how they could fund themselves, be an independent nation. Kirsten never knew the numbers in these things, but she was always surprised about how both sides thought they were right. What was it with economics? Nobody could ever have a definitive answer.

She turned to the man beside her and asked him how he was going to vote. When his answer consisted of parts of Kirsten's body, she simply gave a shake of her head. She wanted to smack him squarely on the chin, but that would've blown her cover. But she felt a hand on her thigh and it was moving dangerously upward towards her waist.

'You can't afford me,' said Kirsten, again, keeping another

ear on the conversations around her.

'I think I can pay enough,' said the man and forced his hand further up on her thigh. Kirsten reached down, grabbing his hand and bending back the middle finger in a sudden jab.

'Oh, piss off, love. No need to be like that.' The man stood up, walked off, much to the amusement of several other men within the establishment. Kirsten went up to the bar having finished her double whisky and ordered another one.

'You new around here, love?' asked the barman, staring at her. 'It's not really a place for women.'

'My brother said he'd meet me here,' she said.

'Who's that?'

'Alan John Martin,' said Kirsten without flinching.

'Well, I don't know him.'

'Well,' said Kirsten, 'it's his sort of pub.'

'That might be, love, but it's not yours. Take care of yourself. I'd get yourself out of here quickly.'

'Don't worry,' said Kirsten. 'I can handle myself.'

'He's not the worst of them, the one you sent packing. There's a few boys come in here won't take no for an answer.'

'In that case, they'll be going home singing like a canary,' said Kirsten and watched the barman laugh. She continued to sit at the bar for the next hour and heard nothing of note from any of the conversations. *It might take a while to get into a place like this. I'll have to come back another day.* As she was thinking of leaving, Kirsten felt her phone vibrating. She picked it up, looked at it and tried hard not to show too much surprise.

'You alright, love?' said the barman.

'It's my brother,' said Kirsten, reading the message. 'He's not coming.' What the message actually said was *Dom and Carrie Anne involved in incident, presence required immediately.* The message was from Justin.

'Did you see the other day that scum got taken out, didn't he?'

'What scum?' asked Kirsten.

'Macritchie,' said the barman.

There was a voice from behind him, a cheer. 'Bastard Macritchie, send him bloody packing,' said a man.

'My brother doesn't like him.'

'He doesn't have to like him anymore,' said the barman. 'The wee bastard's dead. Got him well and true, I heard.'

'What do you mean?' asked Kirsten. 'Dead is dead.'

'Oh, no. They messed about with him first. Just what I heard, of course.'

Kirsten nodded, drunk the last of her drink and walked out of the bar. As she opened the door, she heard a cry from the barman.

'By the way, love, you're welcome here anytime. Much better to look at than any of this shower.'

Kirsten gave a laugh and paced out of the door. Somebody was killing politicians. What was the status with Dom and Carrie Anne? She felt her heart beat a little bit quicker, but she'd have to wait before contacting Justin, wait until she was on the bus, away from this area.

Chapter 04

Dominic sat in the car, eating his chips, watching the house from some distance. Beside him, his blonde-haired colleague, Carrie Anne, was delicately breaking the batter off a fish and eating only the inside. It hadn't been her choice to run to the chippy, but Dominic said he was starving and so paid the penance of actually making the trip while Carrie Anne had focused on the house. Dom noticed that she really detested the onion rings, rubbing her fingers as if the fat had drained onto them. In truth, he'd only ever seen her eating salads and healthy foods when they worked together, but frankly, tonight he didn't care. He was tired and he wanted something that would fill him up, not something he could feel good about.

The pair of them had been watching the house of Jennifer Galson all day. The MSP had made her way back home around about four o'clock, but her kids had made it in earlier while her husband had worked from home all day. Several times Dominic had skirted around the rear of the house and every time he'd made his move, he'd seen nothing. So far there was nothing untoward, and personally, he thought that they were probably on a hiding to nothing with this job. They would wait and no one would come and in two days' time, the boss would bring them back to the Inverness headquarters, advising of their next move. Of course, that didn't mean he could just sit there scrolling through his phone, checking his Facebook messages. Instead, he was the consummate professional, keeping on the move, watching those that came and went.

The night had brought its darkness. Dom had gone and got the tea and now as they were finishing up, the pair of agents prepared to decide who was taking the first part of night shift.

'You look tired, Dom. Why don't I do it?'

'I'd rather push on through then get away from here about one in the morning. Last thing I need is to go home, have a rubbish sleep, and then come back. The quiet hours are the harder ones, you know that.'

'Oh, you've done more of them than I have,' said Carrie Anne. 'To be honest, I don't know why we're here.'

'You know why we're here,' said Dominic. 'The boss hasn't got anything else to go on. If Anna Hunt pulled her back up here and told her to get on with hunting down anything around the murder that happened, she has to be seen to do something. You can't do nothing. Besides, you never know. This might come through.'

'Well, if that's the case, then,' said Carrie Anne, 'I'll get off home. Put the head down for a couple of hours. When I come back, however, I'm going to be better wrapped up than this. It's the trouble with the cars. They never heat the same unless the engine's on.'

'True,' said Dominic. 'That's certainly true. Don't forget to bring a flask.'

'I won't,' said Carrie Anne. 'And you take care of yourself.'

'You make me sound like an old man now. Go on. Away with you,' he said.

'Au revoir,' said Carrie Anne and stepped out of the car, closing the door behind her. It was then that Dom saw the van.

It was jet black, which was the first thing to raise Dom's hackles. You didn't get that many black vans. Most vans that were used were run by businesses that were determined to let you know who they were. Other black vans would be run by boy racers. You would hear them from miles with the large exhaust. This one was being as quiet as possible. Dom watched it slow down and then it turned into the driveway of Jennifer Galson's house.

Dom picked up his binoculars, staring through the trees at the front of the house. It had three levels, an old-style house with a large door at the front and a brass knocker. Dom watched the back of the van open up. Four men ran out all dressed in black and Dom's hand flew for the handle of the car door. He watched them charge forward, a small battering ram in their hands and saw the door fly off its hinges as they hit it. Dom checked the rear-view mirror and saw Carrie Anne turning back. As he stepped out of the car door, he saw her move across to the far side of the road, getting down low as she approached the house.

He signalled to her that he was going to flank beyond her and come up towards the van. She pointed over to the hedge that ran low across the front of the house indicating she would hurdle it. Dom ran forward, making his way across the road, and saw Carrie Anne waiting, not willing to time her step out into the garden until Dom had cleared the van. Dominic could feel his knees yelping pain as he crossed the road. He really did need sleep, but now was not the time to think about that. He approached the van from directly behind, keen to make sure the side mirrors couldn't see him. He doubted the rear-view mirror could see anything, but maybe there was a camera on the outside.

When the four men had got out with the battering ram, the doors had swung shut behind them and Dom quickly moved up to the edge of those doors. Quietly, he opened one, peering inside, and saw no one in there, but also there was a blank interior screen, meaning you couldn't see the front cab of the van. Dom bent down and moved silently along the side of the van, gun raised up at the window in case anyone was there. Stepping forward, he got close, grabbed the handle of the door, and pulled it open. Inside was a man watching the front door. He suddenly started when his own side door opened. Dom reached in, grabbed him, and hurled him onto the floor.

Beyond the man was another guy, dressed in black, who was pulling a gun out from the dashboard of the cab. As the weapon went to move upwards, the far side door of the van was pulled open and Dom watched Carrie Anne drag the man out, arm around his throat. His gun hand was smashed twice against the side of the van and the weapon fell to the floor.

Dom took his own man to the ground, holding him tight, and then quickly administered a punch to the head, knocking the man out cold. By the time Dom was up with his own gun, running to the front door of the house, Carrie Anne had already burst through it and Dom took the stairs two at a time, weapon in front of him. He could hear squealing from above and kids shouting out loudly.

As Dom moved soundlessly up the stairs, he came across a man standing with his back to him. The man was dressed in black with a balaclava over his head and didn't even flinch as Dom approached behind him. Dom put his arm around his neck, pulled it tight, holding the man as hard as he could before he suddenly saw someone break out of the door in front of him. He was in a hallway, which meant that to either side were doors to bedrooms. When he grabbed the man, he had his back to one of them and it was the one that faced him that opened.

There was a gunshot, but Dom had placed himself behind the man who he had grabbed. There were two thuds, making the man groan before Dom threw him to one side and fired his weapon towards the open door. The man in it spun round once, falling to the floor. Dom followed up, breaking into the bedroom to hear a screaming girl in the bed. Dom yelled at her to stay there and not move. He shouted out to Carrie Anne telling *Charlie* there was one innocent in the bedroom and he needed cover for her.

Carrie Anne came up the stairs in the opposite fashion to Dom. He could hear her feet moving as she was in short high heels. He was always impressed how quickly she moved in them and certainly, Kirsten would not have had these as shoes of choice, but Carrie Anne seemed to balance on the balls of her feet.

Dom moved across, checking the other bedroom, but it was empty, and then began to sprint up the stairs. As he did so, he saw the weapon emerge from behind the banister and threw himself to the sidewall. A shot thundered into the stairs beside him, but he continued his route up, firing as he did so, causing whoever was there to retreat. As Dom reached the landing, he came face to face with a bedroom door, which was open, and the sight before him terrified him to his core. A man was standing with a gun in his hand, holding it to the head of Jennifer Golson.

Dom recognised her immediately from the photographs and he could see she was petrified. Her legs were quivering, and the man held her tight around the waist. There was nowhere for her to run, nowhere to go, but in Dom's mind, something else was annoying him. Four men had got out of the van. One had been shot by his colleague, the other Dom had left in the bedroom. Now he had come up the stairs, one had taken shots at him and one was now holding Jennifer Golson to ransom. That third man was missing. This all raced through Dom's mind in no time at all.

'Stop there or I kill her.' Dom discharged his weapon and the man holding Jennifer Golson fell to the ground never to get up again. Dom knew it was a risk because somewhere the third man was watching. He felt the bullet hit his shoulder, fell to the ground and tried to spin out of the way. His vision was blurred and he knew the wound was severe. As he tried to crawl, he felt like his shoulder was separated and he screamed out in pain. He felt someone kick him in the back, his hand being stamped on and the gun he had held before, being kicked away.

'I'll kill the bitch anyway,' said a voice. 'So much for your efforts, son.' Dom wanted to sweep out with his feet, but the man was now standing over him. If he could hook the legs, he might be able to trip him, might be able to reach, but his body was going into shock and Dom couldn't do anything. He never thought it would come to this, to a time when he'd be taken out. He hadn't had much choice. They'd got to the woman, been in so quickly. There in the van, through the door, up the stairs. Dom swore. *If this was it, it was a heck of a poor way to go out, lying defenceless.*

The man suddenly fell sideways, banging his head against the wall. Dom clocked the bullet that had nicked the man's throat.

'Stay,' said Carrie Anne. 'I count four. I count four in here. Two downstairs, two up, all accounted for.'

'All accounted for,' said Dom, barely able to fight to get the words out. He watched Carrie Anne reach up to her ear, calling to Justin, asking for assistance. She took her gun, placed it in Dom's hand, and propped him up against the wall.

'There may be more coming. We don't know. I will guard the door. You stay here,' she said. 'Stay awake.' She looked over to the woman whose eyes were streaming tears.

'Jennifer Galson, get your children and your husband into one room. Until we get covered, get into one room.'

Dom heard Carrie Anne shouting at Justin for more backup and he fought to stay awake. His eyes were drifting. His vision blurred and from the corner of his eye, he could see the red staining across the shirt that he wore. It wasn't looking good and then he felt Carrie Anne's hands pushing down in the wound and he yelled.

'Good, you're still alive. Don't you go on me. Don't you damn well go on me.' A man's hand suddenly appeared, pressing down, while Carrie Anne made her way down the stairs. Dom drifted off at this point. There was black for a period he couldn't register. Then his eyes opened again, and he saw Carrie Anne's face, felt her hand across his cheek.

'Just hold on. You hear me? You hold on. Don't let go.' Dom simply nodded or at least what he thought was a nod. He may not even have moved. In the back of his throat, he could feel the chips he'd eaten earlier beginning to rise, a bit of bile catching. *Thank God she hadn't gone home*, he thought. *Thank God, Carrie Anne was here.*

Chapter 05

Kirsten stepped out of her car and could see the police cordon around the house. As she strolled briskly towards the building, a yellow-jacketed police officer stepped in front of her, and then calmly turned aside as she waved her ID in his face. It was obvious that the main murder team had arrived before her as she could see Jona Nakamura, the station's forensic officer, emerging from a white forensic van.

Beyond her, a black-haired man in a shirt and tie and a large jacket with 'police' written on the back of it made his way backwards and forwards, scurrying almost, between two areas. Kirsten recognised him as Alan Ross. She'd worked with him on the murder team when she was part of the Inverness police force. Alan had been the same level as she, a detective constable, but he had a few more years on her. She was fond of the man, but there was no time to speak to him. The crime scene was busy with an ambulance still on scene. Kirsten strode straight to it, opening up the rear door and got shouted at.

'Do you mind? We're working in here.' Kirsten looked at the woman lying on the bed and recognised Carrie Anne.

'She's my boss. It's okay,' said Carrie Anne, putting her hand up.

'You want to brief me now or do you want me to wait,' asked Kirsten.

'Somebody came for her,' said Carrie Anne. 'They came for her. We tried to stop them. Dom's been shot. He's off in the ambulance to the hospital. He'll be okay, but he's going be out of action for a while.'

'She's going to be out of action for a while, too,' said the paramedic. 'The arm's broken.'

'Were you able to apprehend any of them?' asked Kirsten.

'Wasn't really a chance. It was full-on, boss. They got in ahead of us. Dom managed to get up. We blockaded, but they still came.' Kirsten could see that Carrie Anne was rattled, and all the time she'd known her, Carrie Anne had always been confident. Right at this moment, she looked haggard, worried.

'Who took the scene from you?'

'Unknown. Someone spoke to me. I think it's your old boss. He was called Macleod, anyway.'

Kirsten nodded. Of course, she'd have to go and see him. Clearly, Carrie Anne was not in a good state. The sooner she got to the hospital, the better.

'Did you get any ID on any of the attackers?'

'I didn't clock who any of them were. You can try the forensic team. I think they've been all over the dead people.'

'You get off to the hospital. Don't worry about it. Rest up. I'll come and see you, or I'll send someone.'

'You're not sending Justin to come and see me. Not when I'm going to be lying in one of those gowns with the back half-open.'

Kirsten laughed. For all that Carrie Anne was in a state, she was clearly able to rally enough to keep that dark humour going that they had.

Kirsten left the ambulance and walked over to the forensic team. Jona Nakamura smiled as she saw her and waved her inside the van. Kirsten looked around to see if she could see Macleod, but the man must have been inside the house.

'Probably best if I go and talk to Macleod first,' said Kirsten.

'This will only take a moment,' said Jona. 'You can have a couple of photographs of those who did the attacking. I take it this is probably going to end up more on your side than Macleod's.'

'He knows now I'm two people down,' said Kirsten, 'but what do you have for me?'

Jona produced a tablet and after pressing the screen a couple of times, she held up a picture of a dead face.

The eyes were shut, but the skin was still rosy in colour. The man had a stubbly face and a wide bridge of a nose with black hair that came down across his forehead.

'Recognise him?' asked Jona.

'No,' said Kirsten. 'Can you send that to me?'

'I will,' said Jona. 'I'll do it right now. I've got another one as well.' Kirsten pulled her phone out and waited while Jona sent through the photographs. Once Kirsten had them, she forwarded them on to Justin with a message in the email saying that he should try to identify them as soon as possible.

'I take it they were well equipped for this?'

'They were. There was also a van here at some point, but it's gone. I'm searching through for footprints, fingerprints, the lot, but it's going to take time,' said Jona. 'I doubt I'll find anything. These guys were all gloved up. Looked like a proper job.'

'But the van was gone,' said Kirsten. 'That means that some

of them must have got away.'

'Well, I wouldn't want to say too early,' said Jona, 'but from what I can gather, your guys took everybody out which means there was a second team watching.'

'This really was a proper job. Not just a couple of have-a-go-heroes. That requires a fair bit of planning. Especially, the watch in the shadows when your own team is getting attacked. We'll see what my guys can come up with and I'll share it with Macleod. I take it he's inside the house?'

'He's chomping at the bit. He doesn't like this sort of stuff,' said Jona. 'Happy with a normal murder. This is terrorism to a large degree. It's not his forte, but he's going to get pushed into it.'

'He might be the best to take it forward.'

'He's worried about the upcoming referendum as well. Jennifer Galson was quite big on keeping the union very prominent,' said Jona. 'I'm sure you're aware of that. You've had your team on her. This won't go down well so you'll have to tread a very fine line, if it's not to influence the referendum.'

'The referendum?' questioned Kirsten. 'You seriously think with dead people about, he's going to give two hoots about the referendum? That's not Seoras. You know that.' Seoras Macleod, during the time that Kirsten had worked with him, had only ever sought one thing, to find the truth, to bring justice for those who were killed.

'He might have to do though,' said Jona. 'He doesn't work in a bubble. There're certain things you can throw off. You can fight back as much as you want, but sometimes you've got to tread the path very carefully.'

'I'm sure he knows what he's doing,' said Kirsten. 'Good to see you, Jona. I'll go and catch up with him.'

Kirsten left the forensic van, made her way inside the house, and was directed to a rear kitchen where she saw a man in a large raincoat and a black tie.

'This is a right mess, isn't it?' said Macleod. 'First Dornoch, and now here. Is this terrorism? Because if it is, it's firmly in your shoes.'

'I don't know yet.'

'Your people were here.'

'Can we take this outside?' said Kirsten. 'We've got to talk about it. I don't want ears overhearing.'

Macleod looked around him. 'This is the force you used to work for. You know I run a tight ship.'

'Sorry, Seoras. It's the way we operate now. Come on. I'm sure someone will find you a coffee.' She saw Macleod's glare but sure enough, when they went outside someone approached the detective inspector with a coffee before asking Kirsten if she wanted one.

She refused but turned to Macleod saying, 'You still got them well trained.'

'I don't even ask for these. They just arrive now. Back to the main point. Does this belong at your end? Is this terrorism? Why did you have two people here?'

'We just got word on the wind. It was a small communique but actually, we didn't think there was much to it and as I didn't have anything else to cover off I put my two here.'

'Well, they're damn lucky. You nearly lost your man. Seems to have put up a good fight though.'

'I've got someone back at the base checking through the photographs.'

'Jona's already done that. She couldn't find anything,' said Macleod.

'We have databases you don't, Seoras.' Macleod shook his head. 'Look, I know you don't like it. I know you're not that keen on the Secret Services but you pushed me into it. You're the one that recommended me for it.'

'I did and you should take jobs like this and take them off my hands. This is going to raise a merry dance. Jennifer Galson attacked. I'm here because they think it's linked into Angus Macritchie. If somebody is going after a lot of union-leaning politicians, then this is going to be best suited to yourselves.'

'I'm two men down at the moment, Seoras. I don't operate with a big force. It's not like you. I don't have the backup of uniform. I have to ask nicely for you guys to provide that.'

'The price for working in the dark,' said Macleod.

Kirsten could feel her phone vibrating. Picking it up, she saw Justin's face on the screen. 'Excuse me a moment, Seoras. I need to take this alone.' Kirsten moved away from Macleod until she was a discreet distance and answered the phone.

'Boss, it's Justin. Identified both men. I've got a number of possible contacts for them.'

'Who are they then?'

'Lee McGregor and James Proudfoot. Both interestingly enough, ex-military. That may have been why they've been recruited. Both flagged up as having extreme nationalist views.'

'They're on a watch list?' queried Kirsten.

'No. Just the tame stuff. Not the one that says we actively need to look for them, but I guess that's changed.'

'The contacts you've got for them?'

'Well, there's a number of them but it's not something you want to share about. The information's come from one of our people on the inside, an informant. They can't let it go out as public knowledge. You could put them in trouble.'

'That's understood. Do McGregor and Proudfoot have family?'

'Yes, parents. They're both still in their twenties. Not long out of the army. Both foot guards though. Not highly trained, but obviously trained to some degree if they've been in the military. Could handle a weapon; I believe, with their record they've probably done searches of buildings and war areas. Infiltration, breaking in, seeking and neutralising the enemy, that sort of thing. They'd be ideal for a job like this. Straight in, kill your target, get out.'

'Good job we had Dom here and Carrie Anne; otherwise, Mrs Galson would be dead. Tell you what, Justin, you give me the rest of that detail. I'll come back to the office and I'm going to work from there. It's just the two of us. Give Anna Hunt a ring. And tell her I might need some extra bodies, depending on where we go from here.'

'Or you might have to put me in the field too,' said Justin. 'I'm hoping that's not going to be a likely scenario.'

'I don't know what's going to be a likely scenario. The referendum is not far away and certainly, Edinburgh and London are going to want this solved pretty quickly. I've got to get back now. I need to pass on some of that information to my esteemed colleague.'

'Roger, boss. I'll see you when you're back here.'

Kirsten walked back over to Macleod and raised an eyebrow when she approached him. 'Got an ID on your two dead people. Lee McGregor, James Proudfoot, both ex-military. I'll send over the information. They've got families, possibly girlfriends. I think you're going to need to look into it and see if you can find any connections to any nationalist or should I say extreme nationalist parties.'

'We have had referendums before. It's always caused anger, minor things, people wrecking placards, the odd scuffle, but not this. Nobody's gone and actually killed people for it.'

'It's what it's coming to, isn't it? It hasn't happened for the nationalists. There's been a great sway of expectation previously. Somebody gets the idea they've got to force it. That's what someone's doing, isn't it?'

'It looks like it,' said Macleod. 'It really does look like it. Am I getting the whole story from you?'

'What do you mean?' asked Kirsten. She tried to look Macleod in the face. Like many people, she found it hard to lie to her former boss.

'I've worked long enough with the services to know you don't tell everything. Am I running this case or are you?'

'You're on this,' said Kirsten. 'You take it and run with it.'

'Why me?'

'Because I'm undermanned,' said Kirsten. 'I have two down already.'

'From this level of violence, you want me to simply just put unarmed police officers in? No, you're not making any sense,' said Macleod. 'Don't lie to me.'

'Look Seoras, there's things I can't tell you. You know that.'

'Why not? Why can't you tell me on this? We need to get to the bottom of this for the national interest.'

'There's things I know that if you knew, you would put people in harm's way.'

Macleod turned away from her and she could feel his anger. He swung back. 'So, what then? It just dumps on me?'

'You probably need to be seen taking this. Where I've to go,' said Kirsten, 'I can't make it public. I can't be seen to be doing things.'

'But you're going to keep in contact? I'm going off here to start investigating families, and I reckon it's going to be a dead loss. I think the thing that I need to get on in this case, you've got and you're going to run with it.'

'You know I can't confirm or deny that, Seoras. You know I can't say anything else.'

'If I'm upfront in this, they will come. All the news will be on me to find something. If it goes wrong, it'll fall on me, because I'm the public figure, now. "Inspector Macleod is investigating; Inspector Macleod's on the case." You want me to make a public show of this? You want me to step out? Fine. I'll do that,' said Macleod. 'Hear me, Kirsten, you better get to the bottom of this. This better not go wrong because I'm not having this falling on me. If you gave me the information, I could get to the bottom of it.'

'With all due respect, it's yours. I may have to go places you can't.'

'Keep me in the loop. I mean that.'

'Look Seoras, I know what mind you've got. I know how it works and how you can get to the bottom of things, and I'm not soft soaping you with that. If this is terrorism and the way I'm starting to think it is, it's going to have to be dealt with in a different way.'

'You haven't got that long until the referendum. Make sure you sort it,' said Macleod.

'I will Seoras, I will.'

'Keep in touch.'

'Seoras,' said Kirsten, reaching over and touching his arm with her hand. 'Look, keeping in touch isn't going to be that easy. If you need something, Anna Hunt is the one to go to.

Use her as a contact. I'm two down. I might have to go off the radar on this one.'

Macleod rolled his eyes. He shook his head and then he grinned, before turning and pointing across the garden they were standing in, to Hope McGrath, his Detective Sergeant, who was standing on the steps of the house.

'That's why Hope's my sergeant; you see that, because you're trouble.' Macleod laughed. Kirsten turned away to walk off to her car, but Macleod shouted after.

'You take care,' said Macleod. 'You can't fight your way out of everything.' Kirsten turned around with two fists up in a fighting stance.

'You and me in the Octagon anytime,' laughed Kirsten.

'You hear me,' said Macleod, his tone deadly serious.

'Always. Always.'

Chapter 06

Kirsten sat with her feet on the desk, looking at the computer screen in front of her. She flicked through page after page, giving descriptions of the contacts Justin Chivers had dug up, those pertaining to Lee McGregor and James Proudfoot. One contact, in particular, was interesting Kirsten more than the others. The figure was small. The man was bald, wore round glasses and had a chubby face. He too was ex-military, but it seemed he worked mainly in communications, more of a technical type of guard rather than one based on the ground. His name was Derek Carson, and he'd been mentioned several times by some of the deep informants within nationalist organisations. Kirsten was particularly interested in him because he seemed to be constantly on the move, hopping away for several days at a time.

Justin Chivers entered the room and took up his position, leaning on a filing cabinet on the far side of the room. 'I told you the stuff I got was good. What are you thinking?'

'Derek Carson,' said Kirsten, 'he looks like a possible way in. I think we're going to tail him.'

'We?' said Justin. 'You and whose army?'

'You and me,' said Kirsten, 'until I get more bodies here, you're going to have to go work in the field as well. I know you're more than capable of it.'

'Oh, I'm capable,' said Justin. 'I just don't like it. You can't blame me for that.'

'I'm not looking to blame you for anything,' said Kirsten, 'but you are getting paid. As I've been out and about, I'm off to bed for a bit. You're going to take first watch on him, and I'll pick it up at lunchtime tomorrow. Let me know where you are.'

Justin shook his head. 'All right, I get the night shift; I get all the bad times.'

'Get going,' said Kirsten, 'and Justin, be careful. These guys just barged in looking to kill people. This is serious. This is not some poxy little group they're running; they're ready for the real thing.'

'You don't have to tell me how to look after myself,' said Justin, 'I'm more than capable.'

'I know you are, but I've got Dom carried out in a bad way.'

'On that, are you going to visit them?'

'When I get a chance. This is more important at the moment. Besides, Anna should be along soon. Start talking about reinforcements. I take it that you gave her the message?'

'Of course, I gave her the message, and I think she's getting an ear full. She's got London and Edinburgh onto her. The politicians are not very happy. The First Minister, of course, sits on the wrong side of this.'

'I saw her on the news,' said Kirsten, 'condemning the killing of Angus Macritchie on the attack; of course, she will do. She's not in any way involved in it, but in some ways, it probably hurts her.'

'Hurts her politically, but these sorts of things, sometimes they take a weird turn. What they are doing is pushing this idea that we should have an independent Scotland. You even see the flag flying; it was waving on both sides.'

'Have you heard anything else?'

'What do you mean?' asked Justin, adjusting himself slightly. He didn't like to stand in one position for too long.

'Anything minor, incidents?'

'There've been a few with people getting agitated, campaign posters, yard scuffles, but nothing where anybody's died like this.'

'Well, get on then,' said Kirsten. 'I'll see you tomorrow at lunchtime.'

Justin nodded and left the room, leaving Kirsten to stand up and make her way over to the window. The night was dark, and she looked down on the street lights wondering about independence—was Scotland best on its own? *What the heck did it matter?* she thought. Kirsten never came down on one side or other of the independence argument; she never truly understood who to believe when they made their arguments. She knew Carrie Anne and Dom had disagreements about this. Justin, she reckoned, wouldn't go for independence. He was a Union man, but the one thing she did know was that it all seemed pointless when put up against the number of people dying.

Kirsten didn't believe in terror to get your own way. She wasn't going to start believing in it now. She returned home that night, catching a good night's sleep before rising at 8:00 the next morning. She spent twenty minutes in the shower, ten of them just standing there allowing the water to fall off her shoulders. In her mind, she saw Macleod telling her to take care, but she was struggling to understand where his concern was coming from. He was the one who had told her to go into this life. He was the one that pushed her for it, but he was the one similarly anxious for her. Maybe he understood more about the work she did, and she gave him credit for that.

At midday, Kirsten tapped the window of a car before stepping inside the passenger seat, taking her place up beside Justin Chivers.

'He's getting ready to go out,' said Justin, 'but I think he'll walk or get the bus. Been unable to identify a car for him.'

The pair were sitting outside a tall block of flats.

'How do you know he's getting ready to go out?'

'He made his way out earlier to get some breakfast. I overheard him talking to someone about being out and about today, off to some meeting, but I didn't catch where. I actually don't think he's got a car.'

'Maybe he isn't going far, or maybe he's being picked up. Has he made any arrangements, do you know?' asked Kirsten.

'If he's trying to get contacts on his phone, then he hasn't made any calls. That I do know from his mobile activity, but at the moment, my mind's pretty fogged. I've been through the night without warning until lunchtime. Seriously, boss, too much.'

Kirsten glared at Justin. 'Stop protesting; at least you're not going to have to leg it across Inverness after him.'

Justin nodded and then pointed to the door at the front of the block of flats. 'There he goes.'

'Well then, when you take over,' said Kirsten, 'I'll ring you to say where I am.'

'Brilliant. I'll see you then,' said Justin, and Kirsten got out of the car.

She walked at a distance behind Derek Carson until she saw

him run for a bus. She strode up quickly as well, getting on it and sitting some distance from him. Kirsten was dressed in black jeans, with a heavy metal t-shirt and a leather jacket, and began preening her hair, an action she only ever did when she was undercover. The action helped to keep her hair in front of her face, but thin enough so that she could see whoever she was looking for.

The bus made its way across Inverness before Kirsten got off and followed Carson toward a field on the outskirts. As they got closer, Kirsten could see cars arriving, banners up, and she recognised the blue and white trappings of a nationalist rally. It had been advertised days before and there was nothing to suspect about it. A number of police were there keeping an eye on proceedings but remaining well back.

Kirsten picked up a couple of badges and stickers, attaching them to herself to indicate that she was heavily for the nationalist agenda. As she entered into the crowd, there were plenty of murmurs of talk about the death of Angus Macritchie but also about everything not being derailed, that this time they would win through. This time, the vote in the referendum would go their way. Kirsten spent the next few hours standing, listening to speeches from politicians she could care less about. The crowd cheered even when the rain fell but Kirsten could only feel annoyed and somewhat cold.

Derek Carson, however, was seeing lots of different people. He seemed to know half the crowd but most of the time, it was just a simple hello and a slap on the back. 'We're going to get there,' a couple of words. But one man he seemed to say very little to, despite shaking hands incredibly firmly.

At the end of the speeches, Kirsten saw Derek Carson meet up with the man who stood several inches taller than Derek but had broad shoulders and a rugged sort of look. He clearly worked out and was in good trim. Kirsten wondered if he might have a military background as well. The hair was certainly cut short. Keeping a distance, she followed them off to a pub on a nearby estate. Kirsten took up a drink at the bar putting a flyer in front of her and selecting an app to scroll through. Her face looked totally disinterested but all the time she was listening to the two men two tables away.

Kirsten could hear some banal chat about how things were going with the referendum. Derek Carson reckoned this time they were going to get there but the other man was cautioning against it, saying that they hadn't won the battle yet. Then the jukebox came on, and Kirsten couldn't hear a thing.

There was a young man sitting in the booth behind Carson, and Kirsten started making eyes towards him. She got another drink from the barman and one for the young man. Appearing at his booth and asking if she could sit down beside him, she saw his excited look and pulled out a seat.

Kirsten plumped herself beside him, gave him his drink, and asked him if he'd been at the rally. The man indicated he had. Kirsten asked him to tell her all about himself. For the next twenty minutes, she put her hand up behind his neck caressing it, occasionally reaching down and touching his thigh but all the while was listening to what was happening in the booth behind her. It was as Kirsten had started to kiss the man she was with that she heard talk of a celebration. It was referred to as an item, something specific but never elaborated on.

The young man's breath was disgusting but Kirsten was in the right place and she kept egging him on, running her hand across his shoulder, down his arm, up the inside of his jacket, even allowing him to put his hands up the inside of hers.

This was because behind them, Derek Carson was advising that preparations were in full swing. Constantly, things were being referred to as being on time and that the Arabs would be coming soon. Kirsten was getting quite annoyed with the man she was with because he seemed to be wanting to go a lot further with their rendezvous than they currently were. He kept suggesting they go back to his room. Kirsten said she wanted another drink but every time he seemed to get into a hump, she would kiss him again and run her hands even closer.

The meeting with the Arabs was just a few days away. As the drinks flowed on the table behind her, Carson seemed to open up more. He kept mentioning timetables saying that the result would be right. The result would be on time, it would deliver, and then they could celebrate properly.

It was two hours later when Kirsten rolled out of the pub and pretended to suddenly take a phone call. She told the man she was with she had to run but handed him a phone number to ring. He smiled at her. When she got to the door, she looked back, gave him a lingering look before departing. It'd be the last time he'd see her. She certainly wasn't overjoyed at what she'd had to do to hear the information behind her.

Carson made his way back across town and Kirsten followed, wondering what the celebration was. Carson, however, was not telling and simply made his way back to the flat where Kirsten sat in the car outside awaiting Justin coming to take over. As she sat there, she got word that Anna Hunt was on her way up and would visit in the morning. It looked like Kirsten wasn't going to get that much sleep.

When Justin Chivers slid in the passenger seat beside Kirsten, he had a smile on his face.

'What's up with you?' she asked.

'You did well, didn't you?' said Justin. 'One of the guys on the inside was in the pub. He said you and some guy were necking for most of the time. That sort of thing doesn't happen to me.'

'You're obviously visiting the wrong sort of clubs,' said Kirsten. 'Anyway, we got plenty of information.'

'From the guy?'

'No, from Carson. He was in the booth behind me. Didn't your contact tell you that? I was listening to him talk. Something's going down. Big celebration. There're Arabs coming and it's going to be a celebration and it's going to be when the result is in. We need to get on it. We need to get a better date and time for that meeting with the Arabs. That's our way in, Justin. You're probably going to be sat here for most of the night so start thinking about where we get information from. Go into our contacts. People we've gotten infiltrated, see what they can find out and also the place and time. That's what we need.'

'Yes, boss,' said Justin. 'I guess you're off to bed.'

'I'm off for a shower,' said Kirsten. 'Got to wash that young man off of me. Things I have to do for this job.'

'I can think of worse,' said Justin. Kirsten nodded, letting out a sigh. It had seemed bad enough.

Chapter 07

Kirsten entered the white hospital room, which still smelt of disinfectant, and managed a smile as she looked at her colleague sitting up in the bed. He gave a faint grimace, and she could tell he was still in pain. On the side of the bed were several books, a favourite of Dom's, and he certainly had plenty of time for reading because he was going to be stuck inside the hospital for the best part of at least a couple of weeks.

'At least you survived, but you were a right mess.'

'Gee thanks, boss. I really appreciate that, but in reality, I've got Carrie Anne to thank. She did well. Anyhow, I hear the big boss is popping in.'

'Who told you that?'

'Who do you think? Justin, he's on top of everything. Proper little secretary you've got there.'

'He's just a secretary and I'm the woman that does the coffees,' said Kirsten, giving a smile at Dom. 'But seriously, you forget about everything. I don't want you back at the office for at least a month. You take some time out and get better.'

'I had a visit from Carrie Anne yesterday,' said Dom. 'She should be getting discharged in a day or two. She reckons she could probably come in and do some office work.'

'That will be about it. Looked like it's a bad break she had, although she didn't know anything about it from what I gather.'

'No, but she suddenly went to lean on something and had a shooting pain. That's when it came home to her. At least that's what she said to me. I was out of it.'

'They moved quick though, Dom, didn't they?'

'They did that. These weren't amateurs. These people could move. They've had training of sorts, but they weren't top grade. I'm not sure they'd worked together as a team before.'

'Recruited just for that job.'

'Possibly,' said Dom. 'Very possibly and that's two hits. It's a good job your nose was on it.'

'My nose wasn't anywhere,' said Kirsten. 'We got a bit of luck and picked up a loose end. I just needed you to cover the information while we waited for something to happen. We were in the right place at the right time. Lucky enough for Mrs Galson.'

'You got anywhere since?' asked Dom.

'Yes, I have, but now is not the place to discuss it.'

'Of course not,' said Dom. 'Still good to see you, boss. Be careful on this one. I do think they know what they're doing.'

Kirsten nodded and heard the rap at the door behind. She turned, saw the door open, and a woman in a smart black skirt, jacket, and white blouse strode in giving a quick look towards Dom and then giving Kirsten a flick of the head indicating she should come outside to the hallway. Anna Hunt was never one for a lot of words, but Kirsten felt it was a bit too much to ignore Dom in such a way.

'He'll be out for a month.'

'That's what happens when you get shot, young Dominic,'

said Anna. 'Try not to let it happen next time. Good to see you still alive though.' With that, she walked out of the room.

'We've got enemies, but they're nothing to our friends.'

Kirsten laughed at Dom's comment before making her way out into the hospital hallway.

'Two down, you said.'

'Yes, two down,' said Kirsten. 'Carrie Anne can come back into the office but the arm's broken. She's going to have to take time. Let it set and heal. I reckon she's out for a month, Dom, at least a month, if not a couple more provided there's no complications.'

'You need some backup then.'

'Justin might need some but the more I'm looking at this, I think we need to get inside. These were two hits, Anna. We have barely anything on them, any of them. It's not normal when we infiltrate. This has been run very tight and doesn't look like it was the same people in both instances either, from what we gather. I picked up a tail. We know there's something big going down, a celebration they're calling it. Given what's going on with the referendum, I'm reckoning this is going to happen once the vote comes in.'

'Well, that makes sense,' said Anna, 'and probably not before. If it's something really horrific, they can actually lose votes over it. It seems a bit extreme though to do this once you've actually achieved victory.'

'Well, the hatred runs deep with some people—never understood it myself. I was born in Scotland. Yes, you can make the arguments that we should be this, we should be that, but I think I'm like most people or certainly a lot of people.'

'In what way?' asked Anna.

'I just want a place to live. I want to get on with things. I want the country to thrive. I don't care who's actually running it. When it comes to politicians, I don't think most listen. As long as everybody gets a reasonable standard of living, who cares where your border is?'

'That's not a view held by a lot of people,' said Anna. 'From what I can see from the TV reports and the reports I've read, it seems that things are getting very heated. There's been a lot of trashing of other people's campaign materials. There have been a few scuffles, some serious punches thrown, and running alongside that, we've got two killings. Oh, and another thing, did you give my name to Macleod?'

'Yes, I did. I told him he can get hold of you if he can't get hold of me. I think I'm going to have to go dark on this one. We need to break through, get involved with the people who are running these things. See if we can find out who's mastering it all.'

'Well, they've run two ops with different people. They're keeping well spread out. How are you going to get in though?' asked Anna.

Kirsten waved her outside and they made their way beside Raigmore hospital, standing in a patch of grass where they could see everyone around them but also know they were at a distance.

'Contact I picked up the other day, Derek Carson. He said there were going to be Arabs. We've got people on him, listening to him. Justin's all over him. When I find out where the meet is, I'm going in. I don't know how I am, but I'm going to get myself involved. It might take quite a lot of work to do it, but Carson is my main point of attack. We know he's involved. Therefore, if we can find out how he's involved and what he's doing, we can sort this out, get in, get under their skin, find out timings where they're going to hit.'

'First Minister was on to me. She's not happy. She thinks this will hurt her own cause . . . and she's right,' said Anna.

'She owes us one anyway; we just saved her life.'

'She says she's very grateful but being grateful in politics doesn't mean you have to actually turn around and repay anything. It's just lip service; the more you work in this business, the more you find that out.'

'No debts, no favours. They told us that in our training.'

'Certainly, amongst the higher-ups,' said Anna. 'Do you want me to send some people in for some legwork? I'll give Justin a call. Tell them to report to him.'

'He's going to need it,' said Kirsten. 'When I go dark, he's running the op from behind. You won't hear from me that often but he's going to have to keep contact. Send up three or four. Best they don't see me either, in case they spot me in an op, but they are strictly recon. Not to act unless they see something is happening, something where life is threatened.'

'Okay,' said Anna. 'It's your call. You're running up here, but this is big. Don't be surprised if London gets involved as well as Edinburgh.'

'Nothing ever surprises me,' said Kirsten. 'But as you're here, why don't you take a trip up to the fourth floor? Carrie Anne's in a side ward. Arm up but getting out today. A wee visit to boost the morale of the troops.'

Anna Hunt looked over, raising an eyebrow, staring intently at Kirsten.

'The day my arrival boosts the troops is the day they sack me. I'm not here to lift morale. I'm here to make sure things get done. It's your team; you lift the morale. Now, if you'll excuse me, I've got a date with the First Minister, but I can say we're making good progress.'

'Well, as long as you tell her that and don't give her any of the details, she will just swallow it.'

Anna lifted a finger and then disappeared off towards the car park before stepping into a black hatchback. As Kirsten made for the coffee shop at the front of the hospital, her mobile rang and on answering, she found Macleod on the other end.

'I'd kindly ask that if you give me a number next time, that the person on the other end is able to voice something of use to me.'

'That's my boss you're talking about,' said Kirsten. 'She'd tell you everything she can.'

'She told me absolutely nothing. Now you're going somewhere with this because I'm not. I spoke to the families of Lee McGregor and James Proudfoot, but frankly, I can't get anything out of them. She never said anything about them either. I knew the fact that they were quite nationalistic in their outlook about Scotland. There's nothing else, but that's nothing I didn't know before.'

'Seoras, like I told you, Anna is your contact. I'm going to be off radar in this.'

There was a silence on the other end of the phone. Kirsten waited, then heard a cough. 'Well, take care then. I'll speak to you when it's done and dusted.'

The line remained open. Kirsten wondered what she should say. She managed, 'Thanks, Seoras,' and then put the phone down. Going dark was something that Kirsten had done before. There were always inherent risks with it. It was easy to get lost, easy to get put to one side, trapped in a situation where it was hard to call for help, but working on the other side of this was important.

Thirty minutes later, as Kirsten cleared her coffee cup, her phone rang again. This time she saw the face of Justin Chivers.

'You need to listen to this. This is live feed,' said Justin. Kirsten found a bench, sat down with her phone held tight against her ear.

'So, we're on then,' said a voice.

'Definitely,' came the reply. 'We need to get ready. We need to pick our team.'

'Is he leading the selection process?' said the first voice again. Kirsten recognised it as Derek Carson.

'You know he wants to handpick; you know that's the way he operates. He did it for the first two jobs as well.'

'I bet he's pissed the second one went wrong. I see she was on the telly last night going on about it. Saying how democracy will not be defeated. Made me choke.'

'Oh well, that's only to be expected, but you make sure they're all there, all rounded up. We start just outside the cinema on the estate at the edge of Inverness. We gather together, spread out, and then we find who's coming.'

'Does he have to do this? We go through two or three contacts.'

'You know why he keeps the distance. He doesn't want anybody near him. The celebration is too important. It's too big to be brought down by one person. Just because somebody over spoke, just because somebody's mum thinks they're missing. It's too important for that. We've got to do it this way. He doesn't like loose ends. It worked for the second job anyway. Nobody's tracing back that way, are they? We didn't know them, those who died, did we?'

Kirsten heard the slight intake of breath before Derek Carson answered in the negative. So, he'd made a mistake.

He'd brought his friends in on an opportunity. The contact that led through. Whoever was planning this operation was right in what they were doing, but they'd been let down. Carson had involved people he knew. It was easier sometimes to have people you didn't know, easier if they had to be removed, whether that be dumping them in a ditch somewhere or actually executing them. Maybe everybody was operating in cells, that had been done before, all through wartime with the Resistance. Leaders having organised their troops in such a way that no one could delve in the whole organisation. This time it seemed the man at the top, whoever he was, was protecting himself in a similar way. It wasn't going to be easy, but this was an opportunity.

'You be there with the van. We all head off. We inform them and then we do a pick up shortly after. By tonight we'll have them all there.'

'And then it's up to him,' said the other voice. 'It's up to him to weed them out. Choose the best for it. It seems an awful waste to me though.'

'What do you mean?'

'I mean, what does he do with them? The ones that don't make it?'

'Those are not questions to ask. We pick out our recruits. We see who's the best for him. We put them forward. He sorts them out on that level. Not you, not me. Don't worry about those things; just worry about doing your job.'

'Don't worry about that.' said Carson. 'I'll do my job. I'll have them there. It won't be a problem, particularly if he's going to pay us well. Cash, like the last time.'

'He pays when he wants to,' said the other man. 'Enough. Been on this phone too long. Will see you later. Nothing stupid, okay?'

'Of course not.'

There was a click on the line and then Justin Chivers came on. 'We got a place. Time to get moving, boss.'

'I guess so. But Justin, just to let you know, Anna's sending you up some extra bodies. Don't tell them about me. Don't tell them what I'm doing. Use them for what purpose you need. Keep an eye on what's going on with any of the intelligence. If you feel you need to survey anything, keep tabs on anything, use them. But everything comes through you. No one else. Anna reports them to you. I'm going dark once I start to follow this lead.'

'Got you,' said Justin. 'Do I expect Carrie Anne in at any time?'

'She's available. Probably in a day or two. She's a good analyst, but she's not fit yet, Justin. This is on you. She's had a traumatic incident; I need to debrief her. I need to make sure she's all right. I know you're okay and I need you on this one, Justin. Keep the fort while I do what I need to do.'

'Yes, boss.'

Kirsten put the phone away, made her way over to her car before driving back to her own flat. She'd need to change quickly, get prepped up for anything she required for the long stakeout ahead. By the sounds of it, those they were recruiting were going somewhere that night, but Kirsten knew she had to be at that venue, whatever else happened.

Chapter 08

Kirsten sat in her black heavy metal T-shirt behind the wheel of her car with a coffee on the dashboard. It had been three hours and she wondered when things were going to move. Surely, they had been talking about that day. She had got it correct, hadn't she? There was a meet coming up in front of the cinema.

She watched a couple of streams of people exiting, the shows obviously finished, and otherwise, everything looked normal around the cinema. The car park she sat in served a large complex of retail outlets with the cinema in the corner, its glass windows striving to show the area inside. It was usually quite dark, of course, if she remembered correctly from the last time she'd been in. Kirsten wasn't a cinema buff. Someone had dragged her along and she remembered being very disappointed that the popcorn had been finished before half the film was over. She sat wondering what to do for the other hour.

A black van rolled into the car park and pulled up across two spaces. Kirsten saw the man in the front cautiously glancing from side to side. He was good, able to check his mirrors and everywhere around him without seeming to be panicked.

Two minutes later, a car pulled up beside him, and Kirsten watched another four cars slowly gather around the van. The man in the van stepped out, several pieces of paper in his hand, and slowly walked past each car. In turn, each car rolled the window down slightly, and he posted an envelope through each one and then, as if he'd simply gone out for a small walk, the man got behind the wheel of his van and drove off.

Kirsten watched the other cars, and they began to take off in a line. She fired up her own car and tailed them until they came to the large roundabout at the retail site. One went off to the left, another straight on, next one off to the third exit. Kirsten found herself following those that went straight on. There were three cars, but almost immediately one pulled off to the left further down the road. Another went right, and one continued.

Kristen would have to pick one to follow, but she could understand what had happened. Orders had been dropped and she needed to see them. She picked a white hatchback to follow and watched as it drove along before entering a hotel. Remaining well back, Kirsten entered the car park of the hotel, well behind the man, and saw him go into the front lobby. Parking quickly, she followed and watched him make his way down to the lift. Once the doors had closed, she ran past and grabbed the stairs, sprinting up them, stopping at each floor to quickly peer out and see if the lift had stopped. By the time it got to the fifth floor, when the lift doors finally opened, Kirsten was out of breath but slowly sucked in air as she watched the man disappear down a corridor. The moment he turned off, she followed him. He came back across the corridor and Kirsten walked on straight past him, turning to a door and knocking it gently as if she was going in. The man seemed satisfied and continued on his way, while Kirsten stepped back away from the laundry room door. Thankfully, no one answered.

She picked up the man's tail again, following him down to another corridor, then up a flight of stairs to the floor above. As he stepped into room 601, Kirsten stole up to the door, listening carefully. There was no movement inside. Kirsten knew she had to get in there, had to find out what was going on. She noticed a cleaning lady at the far end of the corridor and made her way down. She watched the woman enter a room and begin to strip a bed, but she came back out to take a few things from her trolley. She nodded at Kirsten, turned her back, and Kirsten reached out, slipping the woman's pass out of her apron pocket.

Quickly, Kirsten returned and passed the card through the reader on the door next to the room that her suspect had entered. She pushed the door open slightly, set a bunch of her keys down on the bottom of the door so that it stayed open and walked back towards the cleaning lady. As the woman came back out of the room, Kirsten bent down as if picking something up from the floor.

'Oh, I'm sorry. Did you drop this?' she asked.

The woman looked at her card then felt inside her pocket. 'Oh, I did. Thank you. They don't like it if we mislay things, especially things like that.'

'Like what?' asked Kirsten.

'Oh, never mind,' said the woman. 'I shouldn't really say, but thank you,' and she disappeared back inside the room. Kirsten turned, paced quickly up the corridor, and entered the room she had opened. A quick glance around showed it was empty, having been made up, and she spotted what she had hoped for, an interconnecting door to the room beside it.

Kirsten walked to that door and placed her phone up against it after tapping a few buttons. She plugged in a small earpiece and was able to hear sounds amplified from the room next door. There was some heavy breathing from the man. Then he put a tumbler down on the desk and then he made his way into the bathroom and she heard the shower come on. Once she heard footsteps and the door of the bathroom close, Kirsten put the phone down and began to work on the lock that sealed the door between the two rooms.

Unlike the card reader pass that got her into this room, the lock was a simpler affair, turned from either side. She took out a couple of tools and thirty seconds later, the door was open. The room was well lit, and Kirsten saw the envelope on the table. She stepped forward, saw it was open and took the paperwork from out of the envelope. Spreading it out on the desk, she took her phone, and photographed the top sheet. She turned it over and photographed the other side. There was a third sheet with very little on it, but she photographed it anyway, before folding the paper back up and putting it back inside the envelope, leaving the item where she had first seen it.

Then she heard the bathroom door begin to open. It surprised her because the shower was still running, and she knew she didn't have time to get back over to the connecting door, let alone get through it and seal it up before anyone spotted her. She quickly got behind the sofa, lying down and listening intently as the man came back to this larger room. There was a bed in the middle of it facing a desk that was up against the wall, the one the letter had been on. The sofa off to the side was underneath the window and allowed for a small space behind it. As she lay behind it, she felt the man kneel on the sofa. He gave tut, looking out of the window before turning around and sitting on the sofa properly. The TV came on and Kirsten heard him flicking through various channels. He picked up some sort of card and started muttering about what was on the television. Possibly, he was looking through the films.

'That's more like it,' he said. Kirsten lay in the dark listening. Music came on the television, and she heard the man chortle and pass various comments about certain women. She then heard some rather agitated lovemaking as she tried to think of it. There was some crazy music going behind it and the man was clearly enjoying himself before all of a sudden, he let out a swear shouting, 'Only fifteen minutes, and then you have to pay for the damn thing.'

Kirsten heard the man mutter, stand up, and paddle his way over to the bathroom. When she heard him urinating into the toilet, she quickly made her way out from behind the sofa over to the connecting door, which thankfully he hadn't tried because the lock was open. She closed the door and quickly adjusted the lock before the man came back from completing his ablutions.

Kirsten went to go for the front door of her room, but she heard the lock on it move. She raced to the bathroom, quickly stepping into the shower area and pulling a shower curtain across. As she stood behind the shower curtain, she heard the door of the bathroom open, and a man came in, splashing water around his face. He made his way back out of the bathroom and Kirsten could hear him fumbling about in the bedroom.

She stepped out of the bath, shower curtain pushed to one side, and stole to the bathroom door. She listened carefully and heard the man on the bed stretching and yawning, before she stepped out of the bathroom at an angle he couldn't see. Carefully, she opened the door of the room and returned into the corridor, letting the door close as silently as she could. Once outside, she legged it for the stairs and raced down to her car waiting outside.

Once inside, she looked at the phone and began to assess what was on the letter. She saw several addresses and descriptions of people. There must have been at least four here, and there was a time given. Were these the right people? Kirsten wasn't sure, but what she did know was there was a time to meet them. The man would be moving off again inside the hour and Kirsten would follow him. She was peckish though.

The hotel restaurant gave a view of the front lobby, so Kirsten entered inside, asking for a table and ordering a BLT. She wolfed down her chips as well as the large sandwich, before finishing it all off with a cup of tea. She was silently praying that she wouldn't be disturbed as she didn't know how long it would be before she could eat again. Thankfully, it was over forty minutes before the man decided to make his move.

Kirsten noted he had changed now into a smart suit and no longer went out to the car he had originally driven off in. Instead, he was now in a green car, a large family saloon and Kirsten wondered just how many of them he'd hired. She walked back to her own car as the man reached the exit of the hotel. She tailed him right onto the main road running around the edge of Inverness. He seemed to be taking a turn up towards the airport, and she followed him closely until he turned off into a modern estate and eventually pulled up outside a house. Kirsten parked around the corner from the man and watched him from up the street. He sat in his car for at least ten minutes before walking over towards a house where he didn't press the doorbell. Instead, he walked round to the large bay window that looked out onto the street and thumped it six times before going back to stand at the door. Kirsten began walking down the street and watched as the man was admitted by a sultry-looking woman.

From what Kirsten could see in the glance that she gave them, neither appeared to know each other, but they made their way inside to the lounge area behind the great bay window. From the street, Kirsten could see them. She tried to slow her walk so she could read the lips of what was going on, but she couldn't find out anything. Her phone rang and she continued to walk away from the house, picking it up.

'Justin here, just updating you. I can't find out anything else, no other word on the meet for these Arabs. Everything seems to be quiet. I don't think there's that many people involved in organising it or at least it's done in such a way that it's kept well under the radar.'

'Don't worry about it,' said Kirsten. 'I'm on it, Justin. I've been tailing some couriers. They're grabbing people in rather a strange fashion. There're instructions gone out for couriers to go and speak to people who are going to tell them who they should pick up. I'm not even sure they all have all the information. The guy I'm following has just gone inside the house, and I think I'm going to have to get in there and hear what's going on. It's not easy though. There's a large bay window. They can see out onto the street.'

'Well, we're dead at this end, so I think you have to go for it even if it blows it wide open if you get caught.'

'Understood.' Kirsten slipped her phone into her pocket.

She remembered how brutal these people had been in trying to take out two politicians, succeeding with one of them. If she got caught, they'd probably just dispose of her. If she was interrupted, who knew if these people had firearms on them. She'd have to be discreet. She'd have to be quiet, and she'd have to get this right. Kirsten turned around and began to walk down the street again. She looked at the hedge running along the side of the house with the large bay window.

That was her start point. That's where she'd go for.

Chapter 09

Kirsten crept along the back of the house by the hedge that she'd seen from the road. She moved in towards the rear door, listening carefully and scanning all around her in the daylight. She was thankful for the large trees that surrounded the garden, meaning none of the neighbours could look in. She approached the rear door, which she found to be open. The hairs on her neck pricked up and she wondered why it would be sitting open if the woman was in the front room with the man. Maybe there was someone else watching. Maybe the woman had more cover.

Slowly, Kirsten crept under the rear window at the back of the house, peeking up over the lip of the sill, and she could see inside the black hair of a man. He had his back to her, but his shoulders were broad, and his height was above average. Kirsten watched him move across the kitchen with his back to her and saw a kettle being put on. Quickly, she walked to the rear door, realising he was occupied. She opened it quickly, stepping inside and then letting it close again, back to the degree of openness with which she had found it.

The kitchen door was just to her right, and she peered quickly around it. Seeing the man engage with a kettle, and with his back to her, she walked past the gap and went to the stairs, climbing up them. She could hear the voices in the front room and proceeded to a bedroom that was located above them. Kirsten knelt down, an ear to the floor, although in truth, the voices weren't that quiet.

'I see how much you like this girl,' said the man in the living room.

'Oh, she's good. Irish lass. Had her trouble with English too. Very sympathetic to the cause. I think she'd want independence for the farmyard animals if she could get it. Everyone on their own few feet, but she'd certainly do her job. Can handle herself as well. Used to get into a lot of fights, then took it to the street level. Made a bit of a name for herself back home before coming over.'

'How'd you find her?' asked the man.

'You know we shouldn't say that. Let's just say a friend of a friend mentioned her, and when I met her to discuss it, she was certainly up for helping out. She's got a lot of hatred for the English.'

Kirsten grimaced. This was all very interesting information, but she needed to get ahead. She needed a way in to infiltrate the organisation. Whoever was putting this rather elaborate plan together, one thing was for sure, there was a level of security going on where people didn't talk about anything, referring only to friends of a friend. It appeared to be well-organised, and it was no wonder there was little talk of it on the street or through any of the other sounding boards that Justin Chivers had checked. Getting people into these organisations was difficult at the best at times but with these sorts of precautions running, and recruiting of different people for each plan, Kirsten realised that those who were joining must be cannon fodder in order to achieve a glorious purpose. And if it all went wrong, they could dump them without even acknowledging they ever knew them.

'She is aware of the risks?' asked the man.

'We're all aware of the risks. You don't seriously think this is my house,' said the woman. 'All you've got to do is pick her up. Don't need to talk to her tonight. I've primed her, she's ready, she's keen to go. Of course, she knows nothing of why she's there, of what the ultimate plan is.'

'It'll be worth it when the celebration comes through though, won't it?' said the man. 'They'll sock it to them. We've looked down the snout of this for far too long. We'll be free and we'll have given them a good hiding to go along with it.'

Kirsten could hear the woman stand up in an agitated fashion.

'It's not looking so good in the polls. I'm not sure we're going to get it.'

'Don't be daft. This country's not stupid enough to do it another time. Look at Westminster. It's a complete joke, and they've got all our money. We get our money back. EU will want us back in; you wait and see.'

'I still don't think it's going to go through. They'll never vote in enough numbers; people are too easily swayed. It's why we have to do these things by force. It's not easy doing it by force. We can give them a bloody nose, but you can't make a change of a country sovereignty by force. It's not Africa we're in.'

Kirsten could hear the woman yawn. 'Anyway,' she said, 'when you come to meet her, she's called Tara. At least that's the name we're using. She shouldn't have anything with her. Told her not to bring much but to dress pretty warm. But just keep an eye on her. Like I said, she's feisty, and don't be fooled.

She might look small, but she can handle herself. She's done street fighting before. I saw her pummel a man when I went to meet her. Knocked the block off him—didn't care either. She looks like someone who could be easily underestimated, so whatever you do, be careful. Don't give her a reason to run or be afraid. She might take a shot at you.'

'I get it, I get it. So, we're picking her up tonight.'

'I've told her ten o'clock, one of the earlier ones for you to pick up.'

'The address?' said the man.

'You know the arrangement,' said the woman. 'I don't know the address, but I know where the envelope is. I put it underneath the frozen turkey section in the co-op. Small plastic envelope down the bottom. They won't see it. Nobody's buying turkeys this time of year. The address is in that envelope, so feel free to pick it up any time. You got any questions about this?'

'I have plenty of questions about what it is, why we're doing this. I'm not used to secrecy, driving around, dropping off here. He knows this. They know that. It's like a giant jigsaw puzzle coming together. Don't worry. I'll pick her up. I'll get her with a few others. He'll get his toy guards.'

Kirsten wondered what he meant by toy guards. What was the ultimate plan? What was the celebration? She didn't know, but she could hear movement downstairs.

The man in the front room had got up out of his seat and was heading for the hallway. Kirsten could hear the other man in the kitchen on the move as well. She left the bedroom and went to the top of the stairs. From the corner, she could see the front door open and the man from the front room was departing with barely a wave as the woman watched him. The man from the kitchen was behind her, and she turned to him saying, 'Just pop upstairs and make sure everything's closed up. Then we best get out of here.'

Kirsten turned and scanned the rooms behind her. The main bedroom she'd been in didn't have an open window, and she tore into the other bedrooms looking around, but none of those windows were open either. When she went into the small bathroom, she could see the bathroom window was open, just a fraction, and she pushed it as open as far as she could. It was small and she could barely squeeze through, but she heard footsteps coming up from the hallway beneath.

Quickly, Kirsten dragged herself through before hanging down from the grey sill beneath the window. She pushed the window closed, getting it back to the fraction of opening that it previously had been at, and held herself in that position until she saw the window close, the man having obviously come upstairs and finished off his job.

Once the window closed, she quickly clambered down the outside pipework and guttering. Touching down on the ground as she heard the front door close, Kirsten heard the woman say, 'Check around the back.' Kirsten sprinted over to the hedge, enveloping herself within it and watched closely as the man came around the back, testing the door again and looking all around him. As soon as the man had disappeared around the side of the house towards the front again, Kirsten tore through the hedge into the next-door neighbour's garden. She got to the front gate, looked left, making sure neither of the parties from the house she'd been in were there, and tore off to her car.

It was now a race against time. The man had a head start going to the Co-Op's turkey section. The local Co-

Op was barely down the road for Kirsten had seen it in the way in. Kirsten tore off in the car, not sparing the horses for anything, several times overtaking in rather dangerous situations, leaving cursing people behind her. She arrived at the local Co-Op and tore inside, pulling her hoodie up over her head and keeping that head hung low in an attempt to mask herself.

After checking several aisles, she could see her target, the man from the house. She ran along, finding the aisle with the freezers at the far end. Quickly, she strode down to the turkey section before opening the freezer door. She reached in and found the envelope. She closed the door, then turned and scanned, seeing the man coming down the aisle. Kirsten fumbled with the letter with her back to the man. She was opening it gingerly, trying to make sure she could reseal it. Carefully, her nail went along, lifting up the paper, and she was thankful when the lip of the envelope lifted up. She pulled out the piece of paper inside, opened it quickly, and looked at the address: Number 2 Sanchez Court.

Kirsten knew it, knew the flats at the edge of town. Quickly, she folded the letter up again, put it inside the envelope, but she could feel a man behind her.

'Are you going to be long, love? I need to get in there.' Kirsten kept her back to him and turned with the turkey she had taken up before, handing it to him. With her head down, she said, 'Can you hold onto this a minute? I'm nearly there. Is there a date on it?'

'It's frozen. They're going to have a long life on them, aren't they? Of course, they're going to be alright.'

Kirsten reached in and pulled out another turkey. She pulled it upright, keeping the letter behind it the whole time. 'I can't see on it. Can you see that here?' She turned around and dumped the second turkey on the man. 'Read that.' Again, she kept her head down, her face out of the way for fear the man would see her.

Kirsten reached in again, but this time she slid the letter under the third turkey sitting at the back of the freezer. She began to pull it out before the man complained on her.

'The dates are fine on these,' he said. 'They're totally fine.'

'Oh, well,' she said, 'I only need the one,' and turned around and grabbed one of the turkeys off him and shoved it back in before closing the door. Before he could say anything different, she snatched the turkey off him and marched away down the aisle, not once looking back at him. Once she turned the corner, she stopped, flicked her head across, and watched as he searched within the cabinet of the turkeys.

Soon he brought out a letter and marched off straight out of the shop, not taking a turkey with him. Kirsten left her turkey on top of several bags of peas in one of the freezers before slowly making her way out. She let the man disappear, aware that he wasn't picking up his prize until eleven o'clock that night. No doubt he had other people to go to, other contacts to find out where those other pickups were, but that didn't concern Kirsten. She was in there, she was finally in. Tara from Ireland. Small, excellent fighter, feisty. Kirsten reckoned she could play this to a T. All she had to do now before eleven o'clock was get along to 2 Sanchez Court, break in, subdue the girl, put her away somewhere, and then join the ride that night off to whatever the great celebration was. Kirsten wandered over to the small café within the shop and sat down with a black coffee before making a phone call. On the other end of the call was Anna Hunt.

'What's the news then?' she said.

'I've managed to find one of their volunteers. I need to get in there, subdue, and take over her life. Apparently, she's small, handy with her fists, and from Ireland. I think I can do the accent,' said Kirsten.

'Well, what are you going to do with the girl?' asked Anna.

'I want you to come up. I'm a little bit busy and I don't want Justin involved. If you come in and anybody sees you, you're not going to be in any other part of the operation. You can also store her away somewhere safe, interrogate her and find out anything else. Can you do that for me, Anna?'

'I'll be up shortly. I'm only down in Edinburgh at the moment. Speaking of which, they're getting very twitchy.'

'They should do,' said Kirsten. 'The deeper I'm going into this, the more the layers of secrecy. That usually means there's something big being played for. This doesn't look like someone that's going to do a little demonstration or rough people up a bit. This is looking serious. They've killed once, tried to kill again. They may go for the big time.'

'That's what I've been thinking all along,' said Anna, 'but what is the big time?'

'It's the big celebration, whatever that is,' said Kirsten. 'I don't know what it is. All I can say is it doesn't look good. At least we have a way in now.'

'True,' said Anna Hunt, 'but this could be dangerous. You need to be careful going in there. Make sure you don't go in with any signs that can be traced back to us. By the look of it, if they find you're one of us, they could put you down in an instant.'

Kirsten felt herself shake slightly. It didn't matter how long you'd been in this business or what you had to do. Things still affected you, and she realised she was going to be up against it on this one.

'Just get yourself up here, boss, and we'll work out who'll take care of that girl. Then I'll get them. I'll get what they're about.'

Chapter 10

Kirsten stood dressed in black, waiting in a side street around from Sanchez Court. The small block of flats was rather pricey. Kirsten found it strange that one of the recruits from what could be a possibly quite dirty job was living here but if the girl made her money from fighting, especially if it was underground, maybe she really was quite good at it.

Kirsten was standing against the wall, looking wholly disinterested in anything going on around her until a woman in a short skirt and a clipboard turned up. She had a pair of glasses on, dark hair and a coat that looked like she was all business.

'What's the play then, Anna?' said Kirsten, looking her up and down.

'Well, I thought I could get in, say I was from one of the environment groups, talk about maybe the cladding in the walls. That's quite topical, isn't it?' Kirsten almost smiled.

'Follow me up. Give me thirty seconds. Then we take her,' said Anna, 'double team and if she's as handy with her fists as you say she is, we need to be careful.'

Kirsten nodded and watched Anna depart. Her boss turned the corner and Kirsten started to follow her, watching her enter the block of flats then make her way up the stairs. At the bottom of them, Kirsten halted for a count, allowing Anna to get thirty seconds ahead. As she made her way up through what would turn out to be three flights of stairs, she heard a knocking at the top and a door opening.

One thing you could say about Anna Hunt was she could play her part well. Her tone of concern, 'what possibly could be in the walls' was impressive, and the other girl told Anna 'she didn't know nothing about it' several times in a light Irish brogue. Kirsten could hear that the woman was at least engaged. As Kirsten rounded the top of the flight of stairs, she turned the corner and saw the pair standing at the woman's door. Kirsten made way over quickly, then realised that the woman clocked she was coming in at a pace just as she arrived at the door.

'What the hell?'

Anna pushed the girl back into the room, almost instantly. The girl fought back, and Kirsten barged past Anna, copping the girl a fist to the chin. To her credit, the girl shook it off well, reached forward, and grabbed Kirsten by the insides of her jacket before planting a foot into her stomach. Throwing herself onto her back, the girl forced Kirsten to sail over the top, and land on her back beyond her, with a sickening thud.

Before Kirsten could react, the girl had turned and was over at her and began to throw fists down at her. Kirsten could see Anna Hunt just beyond her, wondering what she would do. Would she grab the girl from behind? Threaten her? Choke her? Kirsten was in an extremely dangerous prone position.

Then the hand came around, just a cloth over the nose and quickly the woman succumbed. Anna let her drop to the ground before turning and closing the flat door.

'That didn't go as smoothly as planned. It's often best not to engage fighters, just take them out. She'll sleep for a while with what I've just stuck up her nose.'

'Are we going to get her out of the flat though?' asked Kirsten.

'No,' said Anna, 'I'll stay here with her. You need to get through and get dressed.'

Kirsten nodded and made her way through the small flat until she found a bedroom at the far end of it. She looked in the girl's drawers and changed into several of her tops before finding one that was comfortable. She found the girl's tracksuit bottoms to be a comfortable fit as well and wrapping herself up in a bomber jacket, she presented herself to Anna Hunt who seemed impressed.

'Let's hear the voice,' said Anna.

'Why, is something wrong?' said Kirsten while making a west-coast accent from Ireland. It was a soft lilt, not the harsher tone she'd heard from friends in Belfast.

'Sounds good, but don't get caught out with it, and don't overplay it.'

'Of course not,' said Kirsten, and made her way into the kitchen of the house, going through all the cupboards and looking around. She had begun to look at photographs, trying to memorise the faces that were on them, just in case she was presented with any, wherever she was going. It was hard because she didn't know the woman's history, didn't know everything about her, except that she was a street fighter.

'How long we got?' asked Kirsten.

'Another hour and you need to be down at the pickup point. Maybe we could do a drink before we go,' said Anna, opening up a couple of drawers and finding a large selection of whiskeys. 'You drink the Irish one,' said Anna, 'I'll get one of the others.'

The pair of women went to sit down. It was rather strange having time to kill, and Anna switched on the TV to see what the news was saying. There had been clashes and protests over the murders that had already happened, but there was also a lot of reporting about the referendum, promoting arguments made on both sides. Kirsten saw how her own country was being impacted. There was trouble in most places, and in Glasgow and Edinburgh, things seem to be getting severely overwrought.

Kirsten saw the face of Macleod on the television and watched as he stonewalled every question he was asked. Seoras was up in the firing line and not even running the case to find out what had happened with the murders. She'd set him up as a smokescreen, and Kirsten felt bad about it, but she knew Macleod could handle it.

'He's good, that boss of yours, understands a lot without saying much,' said Anna.

'I'm not sure Seoras would approve of what we do, especially what you do.'

'How do you mean?' asked Anna Hunt.

'We operate so much in the dark like this, just breaking in and knocking someone out. She hasn't done anything wrong yet.'

'No, but she was about to, don't ever forget it,' said Anna. 'If we're not pre-emptive, we're behind the curve and then things don't happen. Things don't get stopped and you end up with severe terrorism. They nearly blew up a ship last time and you were on it.'

'Correction, they did blow it up, at least several parts of it. The world's got mad though,' said Kirsten. 'Absolutely crazy, we keep talking about independence and all we ever seem to do is fight amongst ourselves for it.'

'It's all about history really, isn't it?' said Anna.

'That's easy for you to say, you're from south of the border. Be a bit different if you were watching your own country implode like this.'

'I've watched plenty countries implode,' said Anna. 'What are your feelings on it anyway? You want to be free of us?'

'I'm neither here nor there,' said Kirsten, 'I want jobs. I want life for people. I want people to be able to get on with it, support their families, have opportunities. I don't care who's in charge. Anyway, better go empty my bladder before I'm hauled off into who knows where in the night.'

Kirsten stood and made her way into the bathroom. As she was there, she thought she heard something in the living room, but she ignored it before trudging back in to see an empty couch.

Kirsten looked left and right but couldn't see anyone. She had come through the door of the bathroom, and she was going for a bedroom, but it wasn't open, but she could see the kitchen door was.

'Anna, are you here, Anna?' Kirsten stepped through the kitchen door and caught the shadow of something swinging down at her. She threw both arms up and blocked a bat with her forearms. It hurt, but she dropped her shoulder and ran into the person who had been swinging it. Together they hit the large cupboard behind them, both falling to the floor and Kirsten scrabbled to grapple her opponent. She had the girl's hair pulled back and realised quickly it was the woman that Anna had knocked out. The girl threw an elbow up into Kirsten's face causing her to roll away. As she'd rounded to her feet, she saw the girl in front of her.

'What are you doing here?' she asked in her Irish accent. No longer soft, but a harsher comment.

'Just calm down.'

'Calm down? You broke into my house.'

'Because you're going on a little trip tonight, aren't you?' said Kirsten. 'I don't think you are; it's going to be me.'

The girl was good, occupying a doorway, forcing Kirsten to come at her from the front. Kirsten threw a punch and then tried to swing around and catch the girl with a kick to the head, but she found her leg grabbed, and she was driven backwards towards the floor. Kirsten felt the pain in her leg, but the girl hadn't let it go and was now throwing fist upon fist into the side of it.

Kirsten reached forward, tried to grab the girl's hair, but found herself grappled hard, turned over onto her back. Kirsten realised the danger immediately, put her elbows down and tried to roll. Together the pair rolled across the floor until they clattered into a sideboard. Kirsten kicked hard at the girl's knees causing her pain and freeing one hand. She drilled an elbow into the stomach before rolling away. The girl stood up, seemingly still quite fresh despite Anna's earlier attentions. Kirsten was feeling sore, but the girl came at her, swinging foot after foot towards her head.

Kirsten ducked a few, blocked a few as she was retreating backwards. She realised the attacks were coming towards her head. Since the girl liked to use her feet a lot, she let her connect with a few up towards her own head, each time blocked extremely late. Kirsten brought her in, and the girl kept going foot after foot until suddenly Kirsten dropped, swept her own leg around, taking the leg the girl was planted on from under her. She tumbled to the floor and Kirsten dove down upon her.

She didn't wait but unleashed punch after punch. The girl knew what she was about and managed to drive a headbutt up into Kirsten when she got too close, Kirsten reeled, the girl throwing her off and then turning over on top of her. Kirsten felt a blow into the side of the neck and a quick punch to the face, she put her arms up in defence but she was struggling, and knew she was in a losing position.

Then the girl went limp, falling down on top of Kirsten; over her face was a cloth.

Kirsten looked up and Anna Hunt was standing over her, blood running down the side of her head.

'Why the hell did she wake up?'

'Must not have got enough dose into her; I don't know, but you need to get yourself together. You're going to be on the move soon.'

'Are you okay?' asked Kirsten.

Anna held the cloth to her head, she seemed to be swooning. Kirsten helped her sit down. Quickly, she ran into the kitchen and found some rope and used it to tie up the woman on the floor.

'I'm calling Justin in on this one; we need to get you out of here.'

'No,' said Anna, 'we don't. You're talking about quite a big conspiracy here, something done on the quiet; well, we'll be quiet about this. This is you and me only. You're going in and under. I'm telling Justin I don't know where you are. I'm telling him I don't know where you've been, and sure as heck I'm not going to tell him about what we've just done. Absolute radio silence. You're going incommunicado. Do you understand me?'

It had been a while since Kirsten had been ordered so directly by Anna, but she nodded, realising that she was on her own for whatever was coming next.

'Remember the key thing here,' said Anna. 'It's not bringing these people to justice, the first and foremost thing is to find out what they're doing and to stop it. If we round them up after that, we round them up, but they can't be allowed to do whatever it is they're looking to do. You exercise against that with extreme prejudice.' Kirsten nodded and paused a moment, thinking. 'Where do you think they're going with this?' asked Anna, 'Any ideas?'

'It's got to be big,' said Kirsten. 'The way they're operating, it's got to be big, and this girl here, she's a fighter.'

'Then there must be a lot of dirty work to do. Don't be afraid to do it,' said Anna. 'Don't be afraid, so that your cover is not blown. We need the big play, the big celebration. That's what we want.'

Kirsten nodded, made her way over to pick up her bomber jacket again and went to leave the flat. She turned around and saw Anna standing over the prone body of the girl, blood still coming out of Anna's head.

'Are you sure you're going to be all right?'

'It's going to a trickle now. I've got this; don't be late.'

Kirsten nodded and left the flat. As she made her way down the cold steps outside to where she was to rendezvous, she began to wonder just what exactly she was getting herself into.

Chapter 11

Kirsten arrived into the street, scanning both ways. It was almost eleven o'clock, so it was still busy with people arriving back from being out at clubs on a weeknight or else back from doing the shopping. A few others met between neighbours' houses. Kirsten stood at a lamp post, awaiting her pick-up. In her mind, she fought with the nerves of going out on her own. But it was the only thing to be done to get in underneath the skin of the organisation that was planning the celebration to come.

She knew that Anna Hunt would be watching from above, seeing just who would be picking Kirsten up. Justin Chivers will receive a call, no doubt, a few minutes after with a description of whoever it was, and the search for contacts would go on. As she stood underneath the light, her body gave an involuntary shiver and she steeled herself for what was to come. Life had changed so much since she was a detective; back then she was always walking into situations after the worst had happened. She was never looking to pre-empt them, never looking to infiltrate somebody to break down people's barriers, discover the real truth of what had happened. As she saw it, everything she did now was present tense. She was there to prevent it from occurring, not to work out who had done it afterwards.

Maybe that was a little unkind. On numerous occasions, Macleod had prevented further death by working out who had committed murders in the first place. But she was different. Yet she still knew that if she got it wrong, death would be around the corner. In this instance, it may even come for her. Kirsten saw a black van approaching. The hairs on the back of her neck pricked up. This could be it, because there were no windows in the side of the van.

It slowed as it came to the lamp post, pulled over to the edge, and then stopped. Kirsten saw one man in the front. He switched off the engine, stepped out of the van, and made his way round to the lamp post. He quickly glanced up and down the street and said simply, 'You ready?' Kirsten nodded. He opened the side door of the van, sliding it back. Looking inside, Kirsten could see several seats, and the man pointed to one. Kirsten took up the appropriate position. Her seatbelt was applied before the man took out a blindfold and placed it over her eyes.

'How long is it going to be?' asked Kirsten.

'Long enough if you want to get some sleep. Other than that, don't ask questions. There are other people I have to pick up. When they come in, don't look at them. Don't remove your blindfold. Don't say anything to them. The man I'm taking you to is rather insistent on that. If he finds you have been peeking, he won't be very pleased. He may even drop you off the project, and I think it's something we all want to get behind, isn't it?'

There was a hint of threat in what was being said. Kirsten tried to relax, although she felt a tingling in her stomach. She heard the van door shut. A few moments later, the engine started up and the van was pulling away. At first, she tried to work out if they turned left or right, trying to trace her route, but after half an hour, she was completely lost. Kirsten tried to clock sounds outside, but all she could hear were cars.

Then the van stopped again. The door opened, somebody got in, possibly in the row behind from what she heard. They were given the same advice to shut up and not say anything. The door closed and the van began its merry journey again. This time it disappeared off into what Kirsten reckoned was the country, for there were fewer cars on the move. This could be because they were heading later into the night. It wasn't a surprise when the van stopped, the door opened, and somebody else got in.

As they continued on through the night, Kirsten tried to lift up her blindfold without being seen. The interior of the van was in pitch black, and she couldn't see anything. She closed her eyes and went back to trying to relax. They really were keen on keeping this as secret as possible. The man who had picked her up clearly hadn't known her. He hadn't even been given a photograph of her. All information passed only verbally, only a basic description. Did the man at the top even know her if she arrived? That was something to think about. Maybe he would have a different way of assessing whether she was suitable. Suitable for what? Was she going to be disposable when she got there? Were they being picked in this way because the man at the top knew there was a likelihood that these people wouldn't survive? Therefore, they couldn't be traced back to him. Her mind was awash with these thoughts as the van continued through the night.

It was hard to realise the amount of time that had passed, but

Kirsten thought it must now be three or four in the morning. All she'd heard from those who had joined her inside the dark van was the occasional cough, a swallowing, and the move of a nervous foot as it tapped on the floor of the van. This time when the van stopped and the door was thrown open, nobody got in. Instead, the driver announced that everyone could take off their blindfolds. Kirsten opened her eyes and immediately had a torch shone in it. The beam swept through the van.

'Good. Nobody's been daft, everybody's just got on. I say this could almost be a perfect delivery. Now, if you kindly follow me, I'll show you to somewhere where you can get some sleep. You'll meet Mr. Darcy in the morning. He'll be leading you through what's ahead. Until then, all you've got to do is not say a lot to each other. Don't ask who you are. Don't share information about each other. Now if you follow me, we'll be going into this house.'

Kirsten jumped out of the van and looked around, but there was darkness everywhere except for the house ahead of them. The house was dimly lit, but she could tell it was large, like an old farmstead, while the driveway beneath their feet consisted of poorly compacted stones. It was roughly done. *Not a proper job*, she thought.

Kirsten trudged across the gravel to make her way in through the front door. The house, when she got close, had white paint on the outside, much of it flaking. She entered a hall that was barren, except for wooden floors. There were no pictures on the wall, no decoration at all, simply pale walls done in the dreariest of paints.

'No looking around,' said the man. 'Keep going. Upstairs, please.'

Kirsten followed the man upstairs, noting that the people

with her continued. She did a headcount of nine people and was the first to enter behind the man into what she realised was a bedroom. She counted five bunk beds. The man pointed to one, telling Kirsten to sleep there. He told each of them in turn where they should be with one top bunk being left spare.

'Where is that bloke then?' said the large man.

'He didn't follow the rules,' said the man. 'He won't be joining us.'

'What happened to him?'

'You're not following the rules either. You need to keep quiet, keep your own counsel. In the morning, you'll find out what's happening and how we're doing this. Until then, get some sleep. It's after 4:00 a.m. and you'll be up when dawn happens.'

Kirsten realised she had no pyjamas with her, nothing except her clothing, so she simply kicked off her shoes, putting them underneath the bed, pulled back the sleeping bag that was on the bed, and clambered under it. There was a pillow as well, though the whole setup was quite basic. The room was cool. Not cold, but certainly cool. She pulled the sleeping bag around her and sat looking out at those also in the room.

Many looked to be well trained, well built, although she saw one or two smaller people. There were two women in the group, herself and a blonde-haired woman who seemed to be in her late forties. She looked extremely fit with it, like she could run for miles. It certainly wasn't a general sweep through the populace. Kirsten reckoned these people were picked for a reason. Thinking back to the girl she was now supplanting, she'd been told how well she could fight. Was that a requirement? Maybe her girl was used as a weapon before as well, something that she hadn't mentioned.

Kirsten turned over, trying to get to sleep, but she worried about those around her. No one seemed to be getting out of the bed. Everyone seemed to be obeying, and there was no conversation. It took her half an hour to drift off, and even then, she only slept lightly, awaking every twenty minutes or so, scanning the room to find it no different.

As it was getting close to dawn, Kirsten saw a man climb down from his top bunk. He made his way from it, opening the door of the room before disappearing outside. Kirsten wondered where he was going and decided the follow him, carefully clambering out of the bed and keeping her shoes off. As she looked around, she saw many of the others were asleep. As she got to the door, she listened carefully. Slowly, she opened the door, looked around, and saw the man who had got out of his bed at the far end of the landing. He was making his way inside a room, and Kirsten, scanning both ways, ran down it. The lights were on in the landing, so bright that they hurt her eyes which had not yet adjusted from the dark of the bedroom.

As she neared the door through which the man had entered, she heard a noise and immediately threw herself back into the doorway across from the bedroom he'd entered. Footsteps were coming down the landing and she needed to find a way out because at the moment, if they continued, they would find her inside the bedroom door. She opened the door she was in front of and slipped inside. The interior was dark, and she felt with her foot before touching several bottles. Her hand felt around. She thought she was in some sort of cleaning store for there seemed to be many mops.

She heard voices outside the door and resolutely kept herself hidden. Going down on the floor, she looked under the door and saw two sets of feet. They opened up a door in front of them, both making their way into a room and she heard a gasp.

'What are you doing out? You were told to stay. This is intolerable. This will not be accepted. I think you'll have to depart.'

'Depart?' said the man. 'What is this, keeping us like this like a prisoner? It's ridiculous. I came here to help the cause, not to be treated like some sort of thug for hire. Tell me what's going on. When do I meet this Mr. Darcy?'

Realising that the people on the landing had gone inside the bedroom to confront the man who had left the bedroom, Kirsten stepped out of her cupboard onto the landing, and listened carefully at the door of the bedroom.

'You don't speak like that here,' said a woman's voice. There was a thwack as she struck the man across the face. Kirsten heard a kerfuffle before the man was on the floor and she could hear him writhing in pain.

'Best make sure none of the others have jumped out of there.'

As soon as Kirsten heard the comment, she turned, sprinted back down the landing, and entered the door to the bedroom she'd been in. She snuck quickly past the bunks before throwing herself into the lower bunk. As she did so, the door of her bedroom opened. She rolled over, trying to pretend she was asleep, but she heard the footsteps of a woman coming along. She was light on her feet, but Kirsten could smell the perfume from her. Slowly, the woman was making her way around the room, and Kirsten tried not to flinch but to control her breathing into that steady, rhythmic course that the body takes during the night when it's asleep. It was like she could sense the woman's presence, especially once she heard those footsteps get close. The woman was only two feet in front of her, staring down at her. Had she known Kirsten had been out? Had Kirsten given away some sort of clue? There was nothing to do except sit and ride this out. It was thirty seconds before there was a tap on her shoulder. Kirsten made a moan, shook her head, and opened her eyes. Instinctively, she put up her fists.

'No, no. No need to take that action. I'm just checking you hadn't been anywhere. Have you seen any of these people being out?'

'No,' said Kirsten. 'I haven't seen anyone go. Not that I've been awake that often.'

'Are you trying to tell me you've slept right through?' asked the woman.

'No, of course not,' said Kirsten. 'In truth, I'm a little bit nervous about what's going on. I struggled to sleep, but I've only had twenty minutes at a time.'

'Good. You should be nervous. It's a big undertaking you're about to do. Well, go back to sleep. We'll talk to you in the morning,' and the woman looked at the watch on her wrist, 'though that won't be far away.'

Kirsten nodded, closed her eyes, and listened intently until she could hear the feet stepping away quietly and leaving the room. In the next hour, the man did not return to the room. He had left looking to find out things, and now he was missing. Kirsten wondered what they would do. Take him in a van and just drop him off somewhere? After all, he didn't know anything. Or would they do something else, something else to keep him quiet? There was nothing Kirsten could do. Here she was on her own, and her key mission was to make sure whatever plot was being hatched didn't occur. It was now in the dark that she felt truly alone.

Chapter 12

Kirsten opened her eyes to see a room that was dimly lit by light coming through the window. The dawn was just rising, and someone had stepped into the room. She stared through the darkness, and then heard a thump, a clanging sound that continued and continued, assaulting her ears.

'Everyone, get up,' shouted the man, rattling a tin spoon inside a saucepan. 'Time to get up and to shower. Follow me now.'

Kirsten rolled out of bed, pulled her shoes on, and made her way along with the rest of the group behind the man with the saucepan. He led them across the landing she had gone down the night before, around to another wing of the house, before taking them through a door, inside of which was a large wet room. Kirsten could see a line of showerheads, and around each was a reel that supported a curtain which was neatly folded back.

'These are your showers. Everyone will have one, then you will kindly wait outside this door before I take you for breakfast. There are towels over there on the floor, the shower gel and shampoo are with the shower.'

'These are not women's ones?' asked a girl at the back of the group.

'These are the showers. Get showered, then wait outside. I only ask you to do as instructed.' The girl looked over at Kirsten, shaking her head. The man with the saucepan walked past the girl, pointing over his shoulder on the way out. Clearly, he was not keen on an answer.

Several of the men made their way to the far end, and Kirsten saw them start to strip off before stepping inside the shower. Many obviously thought themselves to be in quite good shape, or maybe they were just following what they'd been told. No one said anything about the man missing from the night before. Kirsten wondered. *Had they seen him go, or were they all too scared to ask?* She thought it better than to speak of him.

Kirsten stepped forward to the shower, and calmly stripped off before stepping inside, pulling the shower curtain around her. She showered quickly, but made sure she did give herself a good soaking. Her shoulders thanked her, for the bunk bed she had slept on was hardly luxurious. By the time she exited and took her towel, she was feeling better.

Due to the close proximity, there were many glances exchanged between those within the wet room, but for any man that looked towards her, Kirsten gave a hard stare. She wasn't ashamed of her body, despite heavy bruising, but she certainly wouldn't have chosen to come into a place like this. She was modest, discreet, but the one thing she was finding here was everything seemed to be very functional. There was no delight from those who had led them into the showers or the women's plight at being in the same showers as the men. He had simply led them to the showers. Higher agendas were obviously being sought and Kirsten decided to play the game.

From stepping into the shower to standing outside, she had taken less than fifteen minutes. Others were taking longer. When the woman who had complained came back onto the landing, she gave Kirsten a stare and a shake of her head. Kirsten shrugged her shoulders and looked the other way. If they wanted people who were detached from those around them, Kirsten would give them that.

About five minutes later, the man with the saucepan returned and made his way down to the ground floor of the house. The group was led into a large dining room with benches. At the side were tables where there was porridge, croissants, bread, and other foodstuffs for breakfast. The man pointed over and told everyone to be fed and ready to go in fifteen minutes. Kirsten took some of the porridge and a croissant back, eating it steadily, not wanting to show the hunger she was feeling. The porridge was lukewarm, the croissant, stale, but it was all food, and she felt the better for it. She grabbed a glass of water and drank quickly. By the time fifteen minutes was up, she was ready to go again, while others were struggling to finish off.

'Up,' shouted the man. 'Through here, follow me now.' The group wearily stood up and followed the man out a set of double doors at the rear of the room, out into another courtyard, and then beyond. The day was misty with a drizzle in the air. The man led them through a large wooden gate, and Kirsten could see moorland beyond it. There seemed to be a marked-out area with tape, encompassing a space maybe the size of a football pitch. It was then that she looked to her left and noticed another group arriving. To her right was a third group.

There were several benches standing before the large marked-off square, and the three groups were herded together, everyone sitting down before a small platform was brought out and placed in front of them. It was then that a wiry individual with blond hair arrived. He had sunglasses on despite the day and wore a green camouflaged jacket over black trousers and boots.

'Good morning,' he said. 'Thank you for joining us. This will be quite the enterprise we're on. We all long to see our country belong to itself again, all long to see our oilfields generating money for ourselves and not being raped by those south of the border.

'We long to take our place in the world as a proud nation, one that stands on its own feet, one who is beholden to no one else. Those south of the border have held us in their grasp for a long time now, too long. We may be on the edge of a great victory to take our country back, but regardless, we will show them that we mean business whether the political means works out or not, for if they don't, we will hit them with such force, and if they do, we will give them a reminder that never again should they subject us. This is Scotland, no one else's country.'

The man turned to look at the square behind him, giving a nod before turning back and looking at those seated in front of him. 'You've been chosen because you are capable of helping me on this mission. We all have a common hatred, a hatred of those who would subject our country. Some of you here are not Scottish, but your country is being subjected to such control and domination by Westminster, that you will stand with us, and I welcome you.'

Kirsten realised that the girl she was replacing must be like that because she was of Irish origin. She wondered where the others were from, and she noticed different skin colours amongst them. A few were Asian, one or two Black, and she thought some Eastern European, but the majority had that pale skin of a Scot.

'There are simple rules while you are here,' said the man. 'You just follow what we say. Someone last night did not. He's on his way home, but because of the nature of what we do, we make sure that no one knows who we are. They call me Mr Darcy, but you will not know my name. The rest of you shall have names given to you later. Until then, you shall address each other by no name. You shall not speak of your own name, where you come from. In fact, it's better if you do not speak at all until the time it's needed to make more plans.'

'I have said there will be a great celebration, and there will be when they announce the result of this referendum. Then, we will show the teeth that we have. But not all of you will be there, for I need you to prove your worth to represent your country. I need you to show me that you are loyal, that you can fight to the end, that you can stand in the face of adversity.'

'When I look at you, I can see that we are varied in where we come from. Some of you have been guards before, brave enough to represent this land, and you have served with honour, but they have not treated you with honour. Instead, you're left with so little. I will never leave you like that because we will have a different Scotland, a Scotland that is free. Behind me, you will earn the right to join me in that. Before you, you see a large rectangle of moorland. In the past, so much of Scotland was fought for over moorland, knee-deep in the bogs, fighting the scum that came up from the south. Sometimes, some of our own even worked with them. Some of them still do. In the past, we never vanquished them, but we will this time. This time, we will stand.'

Kirsten wondered where the man was going with all this, but what really bothered her was he hadn't given anybody any names. Everybody was being told to not say anything to anyone. In truth, each person here was a nobody. If they disappeared, nobody would know who had disappeared. There would be so little to report on. Looking along the benches, she reckoned there must have been the best part of thirty people here.

'Like our ancestors, you'll be able to stand here and to show you are worthy of Scotland. You can't see it from here, but in that bogland, there are many weapons. There are no guns, but there are many knives, swords, cudgels, baseball bats, and other items. You will all be put on the edge of the rectangle and told to enter. You will all enter, but only six will come out. The six that are standing at the end will come out, and they will get the opportunity to fight for Scotland properly. I see some of you are struggling with that. I see some faces questioning. Understand that if you leave that rectangle, you'll be shot.'

The man turned, pointed to one of his individuals who had been there with him, and he pulled a handgun out from behind his back.

'You'll be shot without prejudice, and the game will continue inside. There are no rules once inside. Some will band together, some won't, some might try and stand on their own. I will not intervene in the moorland. I will simply blow a whistle when I see only six standing. When you fight for your country, you must show no mercy. When you stand for Scotland, you must have no regrets or doubts about what you're going to do to our enemy. When the celebration comes, I cannot have those who are weak. You wanted to do something for your country; you wanted to stand and show them. Well, this is it, but first, you must stand and show me what you're capable of.

'Some of you may notice that there are women amongst you. Our women have always fought, too. They say you're the more deadly of the species; I think we shall see that. Men, show them no mercy, for I expect they will show you none either. Now, tip your benches up.'

Several of the men who had come with him urged those on the benches to stand up, and they tipped them over, placing them onto the flat. They then herded everyone over, and Kirsten walked with the crowd where they were corralled together. Kirsten thought things had gotten crazy when the bagpipes started to fill the air, their pipes sounding out, 'Flower of Scotland'. Mr Darcy raised his hands up, encouraging everyone to sing, and Kirsten saw several of the crowd starting to sing gustily. She joined in, keen to show that she was there to be a part of this enterprise, but there were others amongst whose faces showed shock and horror.

When he said they were to go inside this arena where there would only be six standing, what did that mean? Would people be dead? she wondered. She didn't see how it wouldn't happen. *People die when people have fights in bars, and now I hear they will be fighting for their lives, fighting to be the six.* There was something else on her mind. *What'll happen to those who aren't good enough?* She never saw the man from last night leave the house. They just said that he'd been gone. That he failed and was on his way home.

Kirsten had a deep and uneasy feeling within her, and as her face and voice sang heartily, the rest of her shook with the fear of what would come next. What would she have to do, and just how serious was this guy? Was it a test they were being put through? She had seen the body of Angus Macritchie, the politician found dead, wrapped in a Scottish flag. They had shown him no mercy. There'd been no retreat, no surrender.

Mr Darcy started to scream, 'Scotland,' over and over again, trying to whip up his thirty would-be fighters. The pipes blared, and Kirsten yelled, throwing her hand into the air, shouting out, 'Scotland,' for all she was worth, but across from her, she could see the tears on a man. He didn't look that strong, and he didn't look very old, but tears were running down his face. They were not tears of excitement; they were not tears of passion. Instead, they were tears of fear. And as she watched, his trousers started to dampen.

Chapter 13

Anna Hunt had endured a busy night. Once Kirsten had left the flat, she'd had to take the young lady in question to a safe house away from everyone else and then pick out an employee who could look after her without being missed by the rest of the organisation. The young employee came quickly once Anna had called her but it was still four in the morning by the time Anna had departed.

The house was out in the hills and the subject was to be held sedated by the use of drugs. She made sure the surrounding area was clear before Anna made her way back into Inverness. The lights were on upstairs at the base of Kirsten's unit. Anna had a key to get in through the front door as the shop down below—that usually gave cover as to what the offices above were for—was closed at that time.

Anna climbed the stairs to find an office with one light on. Inside on the left, by the light of a computer, was Justin Chivers, his hands moving across the keyboard at a rate of knots that always bamboozled Anna. Her mind worked at that speed, but the digits of her fingers were never able to achieve such a pace.

'Boss, wasn't expecting to see you. Have you heard from Kirsten?'

Anna Hunt strode into the centre of Justin Chivers's office, looking immaculate as ever. Her skirt, which dropped just below her knees, had barely a mark on it. The jacket that she wore was buttoned up. The dark material gave a seriousness to her look that was matched by her face.

'I believe Kirsten told you she was going off-grid. Said you were to look after the office.'

'Correct,' said Justin.

'So, what are you doing?'

'Well, it'd be a lot easier if I knew where she was going. I've been chasing up the contacts that she made, but she headed off to find new ones and she hasn't called back yet. She said she might be some time.'

Anna Hunt walked slowly in front of Justin's desk and put her hand over the top of his computer screen making sure she had his attention.

'Kirsten may not be back until this is all over,' she said. 'With that information, understand that you're running up here. I have given you several people in this list,' said Anna, throwing an envelope onto the table. 'You are to communicate with them, use them for what you need. Find out what you can, but you talk to me.'

'Where is Kirsten now?' asked Justin.

'That's on a need-to-know basis and you do not need to know that. When she's ready, she'll contact, not before, but we need to get on the ball, Justin. She may contact in odd ways. Your people may also see her in the field. Therefore, no one gets to know who she is. Don't talk about the boss with the people I send you. They won't know her; they won't know what she looks like.'

'Okay,' said Justin, watching Anna carefully. 'Do you know

that something big is going on?'

'I know what you know,' said Anna.

'I doubt that very much,' said Justin. 'I've worked with you for too long to believe that.'

'*Touché*,' said Anna. 'You know what you need to know, but we need to know more. There's to be a celebration—that's what we know. Let's presume it's an attack. We need to find out where and when.'

'I've got all the sources out,' said Justin. 'There's not a lot more I can do.'

Anna turned on her heel, marched across to the coffee pot, and felt the side of it. She realised it was warm, took a mug and poured some black coffee into it.

'There's always more we can do, Justin. How's Carrie Anne?'

'She's talking about coming in, in the morning. I think her arm's quite bad though. Sore.'

'Does her mind work?'

'Yes, she says she's good to go in that department.'

'Then get her in. Get her going through who we know on the nationalist side. Use her to coordinate the people I've given you. She's a good analyst. She can sift through the information.'

'Of course. I will,' said Justin. He stared down in front of him. 'You okay?'

'Of course, I'm okay. What type of question is that?'

'You seem a little bit tense, apprehensive. First thing to look after yourself. You know that, don't you?'

'Of course, I know that. You forget I was with her on the ferry when we took the man down. We saw her deal with a bomb on a boat. I know she can handle herself. That's why I gave her this job.'

'Yet you still look worried,' said Justin.

'I'm worried because I have no way of contacting her. I don't know where she is at. She walked blind into this. She's got no equipment with her except herself and I'm waiting for her to contact. We've got a referendum up. A terrorist attack could blow Scotland into a national catastrophe where you have the guts of a civil war going on. Certainly, plenty of violence in the street. Yes and no campaigners at each other's throats and not just the normal bickering, so yes, Justin, I'm pretty worried.'

'Well, I guess that's fair enough,' said Justin, 'but the boss will come through. She always does.'

'There seems to be a harshness to whoever's doing this,' said Anna. 'We've heard nothing back, next to nothing about what's going on. Usually, you hear things on the mill, but somebody is keeping such a tight lid on this. That's why I let her go off, that's why I let her get involved in it but I'm telling you now, I'm not happy, Justin. I've got Edinburgh on my neck saying we want the perpetrator of the killings of the politicians brought forward and we have nothing to show them.'

'We have a couple of people.'

'We don't have who's doing it. The only people we have framed for doing the job are dead. We've got very lucky with a lead and all I have is Kirsten chasing that down. You need to find me something else, Justin. You need me to find something else so I can be there for her when it all starts to happen.'

'So that's what it is. You're worried when she reaches out nobody's going to be there. You're worried it's going to happen too fast.'

Anna Hunt walked over to the window, stood looking out at the orange street lamps, the drizzle coming down slowly. 'You're right. I'm worried,' she said. 'I'm very worried.'

* * *

'Remember, no one is important. Just a cause we fight for.' Mr. Darcy was standing up on a platform addressing the group again, after enchanting them by singing nationalist songs and anthems. He had settled them down again, staring at them. It felt as if he was looking at each one individually despite the number of people he had to scan with his eyes. Kirsten was standing in the middle of the group watching him closely, looking for any clue as to who he was or even to where they were at the moment. Clearly, they were up in the mountains, but she didn't recognise this place.

'I need to tell you a story about loyalty,' said Darcy. 'Look over here.' Kirsten saw him point to the man who had driven her in the van the previous night.

'A number of you were picked up by this man. I'll not tell anybody any names. Of course, I won't, but you need to understand that we have known each other from birth. We fought for independence together for years. I have stood with him on numerous rallies, I have caused disruption to try and get this country back with him by my side. When we planned this, I did it with him. We planned the death of that traitor, Macritchie, and we planned it together. I planned the death of the rat Galson only for her to survive, but we did all this together. I trusted him to go and round you up, all the while making sure that he didn't know your names, that you didn't know his.

'I don't even know the names of some of you, because the only thing that's important is the mission. My friend persuaded me to go back out and be useful but he has driven around now, picking you all up. He knows where he collected you all from. When it comes to this mission, he is a danger for he can tell me exactly where nine of you came from. Is that not true?'

There was a murmur amongst the small group. Kirsten was aware that their minds were suddenly working out what was going to happen to this man.

'Come here my friend, come here.'

Mr. Darcy stepped forward, and the man who drove the van embraced him. They hugged together, tightly, and then stepped back looking into each other's eyes. Kirsten could see the friendship. She could tell the hours they'd spent together, working on common goals.

'And the lesson I am to teach you was that nothing is more important. Friendships, money, your family, nothing is more important than the mission we go on. The mission cannot be allowed to fail. That is why the locations you were picked up from have to be removed from memory.'

Suddenly, Darcy whipped out a handgun, pointed it at his friend standing three feet away, and without hesitation, he shot the man dead. Kirsten watched the body fall backwards, saw that many of the group amongst her shrieked in horror, buckling over.

'And that is the dedication you have to have. That is what you have to show me. We are going to do a most momentous act, but no one can know until it is the time and even then, we have to act correctly. We have to sacrifice to get what we want, for the good of the mission is the only thing.'

Kirsten saw the body lying on the ground in front of Darcy. She couldn't believe it was his friend as Darcy turned around waving at a few of his other guards to take away the body now lying there.

'Dear God,' said somebody.

'God does not come into it. Your faith, your religion, nothing comes into it. Only doing what needs to be done for this country. Do you all understand me?'

There was a shocked silence and Kirsten could see that Darcy was not pleased with it.

'I said, do you all understand me?' This time there were a few murmurs, but Darcy asked a third time, 'Do you not understand me?' This time there was a half-hearted cheer, but it was clear that not everyone expressed it. 'You will understand me,' he said, 'and you'll understand me right now. Take them out and bring them to the rectangle. I want to see them all together.'

Darcy's men moved towards the group pointing guns at them and herding them around the rectangle. Kirsten found herself moved to the far end, but in doing so she had to trudge across the moorland. Every now and again her feet would drop severely, and she was struggling to find solid ground on which to stand. As she reached a corner, she was told to stop, and looking to her left, she saw a large man, some six foot six tall, muscles, someone who looked like a bouncer. To her right was a lithe man. He looked fit, younger than her.

'That's it,' yelled Darcy. 'Gird yourselves. Be ready for this. You do this for Scotland. When I give the order to step inside the rectangle, you will enter and you can do what you want at that point, but only six of you walk out. Anyone that is not inside the rectangle within five seconds of my command, we will shoot.'

Kirsten looked around her. There were some thirty people about to enter in a mass free for all. Yes, there were weapons on the ground; ahead of her she could see some. A sword was sticking out of the ground. Possibly, there was a knife ahead. Was that a pair of knuckle dusters on the floor? Even in the distance, she could see a mace. What madness had she walked into?

'It is now time. Now time for you to achieve your worth. Show Scotland you deserve the right to punish those south of the border. Enter now. Enter now.'

Darcy blew a whistle. The shrill noise was a flame through the air. Kirsten could feel herself begin to shake. The big man to her left moved through the barrier and began running forward, hunting for a weapon on the ground. The lithe man to her right disappeared in also. Kirsten found herself frozen. She glanced along the line where everyone had seemed to go in and saw one of Darcy's guards pointing a gun at her. She took two steps forward, bending under the tape that ran around the area. She was now inside, and she would have to fight.

Chapter 14

Kirsten was unsure what to do. Clearly, she was going to have to fight for her life, but the people opposing her hadn't asked to be there. She was capable of using lethal force, although in truth, she'd only ever really used it with her weapon in her hand. She'd shot people who were coming to injure her or possibly kill those she was protecting, but these people were just cast into what was a right mess. Most criminals you came across, even terrorists, wouldn't dream up such a thing as this. Darcy, whoever he was, was clearly off his rocker, but that couldn't be sorted now. All she could do was deal with what was in front of her. She'd try and knock them out, try and down them without killing them. That was the right thing to do, wasn't it? Was it?

How could you apply any rules to this situation? They didn't train you for this. They trained you for evil people coming at you, but not this madness. A part of Kirsten wondered what Darcy's real plan was behind it all. Was he simply a nut wanting to do anything to further the idea of independence, or had he something to gain from independence? She didn't recognise him, didn't know him from public life, and she was pretty good with all the major figures.

Kirsten seemed to be the only one standing, looking around, assessing the situation. Everyone else had simply made off for the nearest weapon. The man who had been standing beside her, the massive giant over six foot, had picked up a weapon and now turned to look back at her. Kirsten was short and she must have looked like an easy target. No one here would've known that from the age of ten, she started training inside a mixed martial arts ring. No one would know that she spent many hours grinding away, working through the pain barrier, so she could fight in such an octagon. No one would know that she was reasonably successful. To them all, she looked like a small woman who, while being in reasonable shape, certainly didn't have the muscles to justify being a threat.

Her interior muscles were well hidden, and the fact that she could strike where she wanted and how she wanted made up for a lot for the bulk of muscle that was missing. She could take a punch. She could take a punch and still be standing, still react to it. That was always underestimated. The really hard people were those who could keep coming. Those who didn't stop, those who no matter when you hit them, hit back just as quick. From the corner of her eye, she saw the large man charge at her. His black hair, sleek, his face now red from the exertion of running and in his right hand, she saw a machete.

From the way he is holding it, thought Kirsten, *he doesn't know how to use it. He'll come at me, wild swing.* Kirsten stood her ground, holding a fist out in front of her, a second one behind. After a quick glance around, she realised no one else was moving towards her except for this giant. As predicted, he ran towards her, sweeping the machete round about shoulder height. If he had hit, the blade would have embedded itself at the top of Kirsten's arm. He probably would've struggled to get it back out again, but because she knew it was coming, Kirsten simply ducked. The man's arm swung through and he'd suddenly covered himself up, his right arm moving across his chest. Kirsten did the simplest thing she could, put her foot out, making the man trip and he went face down into the moorland bog.

She turned to follow him, her foot stomping hard down on his hand, causing the machete to be dropped. She dove down on his back, wrapping an arm around his neck, pulling it tight until she could hear him choke. It would've been quicker to assault the back of his head with several punches, but she didn't want to kill the man. She merely wanted to put him to sleep. As she stared all around her, she slowly throttled him until eventually, he dropped unconscious back to the ground.

Kirsten reached over, took the machete, and threw it out of the rectangle they were in. She didn't know how to fight with it. It would be a hindrance, as it was never a weapon she'd trained with. Rather than race forward into more battle, Kirsten stood her ground, watching around her, seeing others fighting in various forms of brutality. She saw a thin man take a knife to the stomach, fall to the ground, while the man above him cheered, before suddenly getting hit from behind by a baseball bat. He toppled down and the man behind him never stopped, simply kept running.

Kristen was also aware that many fell over, trying to move around the coarse ground. One minute you were up on top of the plant vegetation, and then you found a hole and went down about two feet, at a pace that took you off your feet. If you were walking, it merely dropped you down, an inconvenience that could prove costly.

Kirsten kept spinning, turning around. It was then she saw

someone coming towards her. The man held a serrated knife and from the angle of his body, his stance, and the way his hands were reaching out, she could tell he knew how to use it, possibly military trained. She swallowed hard, for this would not be a simple task.

The man came up towards her, but rather than lunging forward, he began to circle. Kirsten held her hands up to her face as if she was panicking. The man began to taunt her, telling her what he would do to her once she was on the ground. What did this guy have against her? The man in front of her was pure evil. The things he was saying about her, the worst kind.

Kirsten made as if to go into a ball, turning her back away from him, but her eye kept him just in focus. Her ploy had worked, for he didn't reach forward in an attack pose, rather he reached forward to try and grab her. She spun out of her crouched position, launching a kick right across his jaw. It caught the man square on and he spun before falling down onto the turf below. He lay motionless, but Kirsten still reached over, taking the knife out of his hand, once again, flinging it out of the rectangle.

Slowly, she moved away from her position because she could see that numbers were dropping around the rectangle. She thought about moving herself away, even further from the group fighting, but she saw a woman trapped. Something stirred inside of Kirsten, for what had just happened to her was happening to this woman, but on a larger scale. Four men were circling her. Occasionally, they would bicker between each other, threw out the odd arm to push each other away, saying who was going to have her first. As Kirsten saw one man move in, she could feel the anger rising inside her. She fought to control it because she was about to run into a barrage of four men, and she'd have to have her wits about her.

A man reached in, grabbing the woman by the hair, and pulled her towards him. By the time he'd achieved this, Kirsten had arrived at the group and had already taken one man out from behind, kicking him behind the knees while pulling him down by the hair. She then stomped on his face, before reaching for the man who'd grabbed the woman. She hit him with four consecutive punches, all to the head, causing him to tumble backwards. As she followed through, another man from the side threw himself at her, hitting her in the side and taking her to the ground.

Most people don't know how to fight when on the ground. They scrabble about, but Kirsten had been trained in it. The wrestling side of her mixed martial arts was coming in as she rolled the man over and from on top of him, drove her elbow into his neck, causing him to choke badly. She would have remained there to subdue him completely, except she knew others were on their feet and she threw herself to one side as she felt something coming down towards her. It was a spear driven at her, but because she got out of the way, it instead ended up in the shoulder of the man lying prone on the ground.

Kirsten got to her feet to face her attacker who pushed the spear at her several times. She jumped from side to side to clear it. She could see the woman was panicking, and the man she'd originally dropped to the ground was now back on his feet, reaching for her. This time the spear came at her, and Kirsten stepped to one side, taking it with two hands, and pulled it hard towards her. The man didn't let go and came with it, only to find Kirsten plant her forehead straight into his nose. The blood spattered and the man reached up, shouting out loudly as he fell to the ground, unable to keep his balance amongst all the moss and heather.

Kirsten kicked out with her leg, hitting the man who was holding the woman, causing him to let go. She shouted at her to get behind her.

'Take the spear,' said Kirsten. 'Take the spear.'

The woman grabbed it and Kirsten could feel her back onto her. Three of the men were back up now, reaching forward again. Beyond them, there was very little movement within the rectangle, and the three men encircled the women. Kirsten could hear Darcy laughing and beyond her, she saw another four men standing together. There was nobody else left in the field, nobody else upright. Just the four men off in one group together and the three predatory men circling the two women.

'Don't break away,' said Kirsten. 'Stay back to back. Then they can't come at us from behind.'

'I hear you, sister,' said the woman. One of the men in front of Kirsten turned around, took steps back, and picked a large sword up out of the ground. He clearly didn't know what he was doing with it. As the man raised it high and charged, Kirsten broke forward, planting a kick squarely into his midriff. He struggled to do anything with the sword as the wind was knocked out of him. Kirsten followed it up with another punch, making him topple to the ground.

The woman, sensing she had moved, moved with Kirsten and as the next two men came towards them, realising that Kirsten had been distracted, the woman poked the spear towards them. One of the men grabbed it while the other reached in towards her.

Kirsten, turning around, saw what he was doing, ran and jumped, catching him round the neck with her left arm. Being off the ground, the man felt the full weight of the arm hit his neck, and his feet went from under him as Kirsten took him to the ground. She punched him hard twice in the face before rolling away to get to her feet. The other man was tugging the spear away from the woman, but Kirsten admired how she was hanging on tight, trying to pull it back.

Kirsten didn't want the fight to go on any longer. As the man saw her coming, he desperately tried to pull the spear back, but he was unsuccessful as Kirsten caught him around the face with a kick from her left foot. The man spun and fell, and Kirsten looked at the work around her. They were all down, but none of them were dead. She had succeeded in taking them out in the way she hoped she would. Looking across the field, she saw the others had not been so lucky. A whistle blew, shrill but welcoming to Kirsten and she sat down on her backside, looking around her. The woman with the spear turned to the men who'd been attacking them and plunged the spear down into the heart of one of them.

'No,' shouted Kirsten. 'What are you doing?'

'They would have had us,' said the woman. As Kirsten stood up to prevent her doing the same to another man, she was too late and the spear went through another heart.

'Dear God,' said Kirsten. 'What are you doing? It's a trial. We're not here to murder each other.'

'No?' said the woman. 'I thought he made that pretty clear,' and she stormed off out of the rectangle. Kirsten looked at the body beside her, the man she'd taken out but left alive. She looked over to the edge of the rectangle. She saw Darcy coming in, clapping his hands and looking at the woman leaving.

'Good. Good, I see we've got some proper fighters on our hands, but you,' he said, pointing at Kirsten, 'you should take a leaf from her book. Gut your enemies. Put them down. You didn't kill anyone. You merely knocked them out.'

'I thought that was the point,' said Kirsten. 'Just to defeat them.'

'You never took a weapon,' he said. 'Not once.'

Kirsten put her hands out in front of her. 'These are my weapons. No point carrying something you don't know what to do with.'

'Indeed,' he said. 'Indeed. Now, all of you, off this field and back into the house. Leave the rest of them to my men. They'll send them home.'

Kirsten looked over the field. 'Some of them won't be going home.'

'No,' said Darcy. 'But they died for Scotland. They died standing for their country. Their sacrifice will be honoured. What they gave will be nothing to the damage that we will cause to those south of the border. We will be free one way or another, whatever happens with this referendum. Scotland,' he shouted, 'Scotland forever,' and Kirsten lifted her fist in the air, bile in her throat, but shouted anyway.

'Scotland, Scotland forever.'

Chapter 15

Kirsten's head was spinning. She'd had no time to think about what she was getting involved in, but even in her worst nightmares she never thought it would be like this. Most organisations, especially terrorist, may have put you through a test of your loyalty, but they would have sent you out into the community to commit some robbery, or possibly even to take someone out. But never had she heard of a group pulling in so many individuals to have them fight for their place. Not that anyone had a choice. Many didn't seem to be willing, although no doubt they'd looked at the blood lust of many of them. She was still struggling with the woman who speared the man in front of her after everything was said and done.

Darcy instructed the guards to drag the unconscious ones out of the ring and he didn't seem to have much time for them. For those who were walking wounded, he told them to ship out, to go over to the vans that were sitting across from the house.

'What's going to happen to them?' asked Kirsten.

'They'll be sent back. They've done their duty for their country,' said Darcy, 'but they were found wanting. Not everyone can be a hero in this, but the sacrifices they've made will not be unheeded.'

What sacrifices? thought Kirsten. *Well, there was a couple that sacrificed everything, because they were lying dead on the field. But the others, the walking wounded, they'd just been involved in a rather bizarre fight. There was nothing patriotic about this.*

Kirsten watched, trying to maintain a detached manner, as a couple of bodies were dragged right past her towards the vans. She looked at those walking wounded inside, some with blood coming down from their faces, and Darcy shouting at them to pick up the bodies and pull them inside the van as well. When he returned to his glorious six victors, he began to shake each of them by hand, but when he came to the two women, he stopped, smiling broadly.

'I honestly didn't think any of the girls would get through. You,' he said to Kirsten, 'you've clearly been trained to fight. A couple of those moves you did, and restrained with it, you didn't look to kill anyone.'

'You said last standing. Even in our street fights, you don't finish them off.'

'Indeed not,' said Darcy, 'but this woman here did. She's got the cold eye. She'd do it. When it came down to it, she'd finish off anyone.' He took a hand up to the woman's face, smearing away blood. 'You could all do with a shower,' he said. 'Take some time to relax. Let's let you get cleaned up and then we'll start talking and training for our great celebration.'

Kirsten watched him walk away, stepping over to several of his guards standing around the vans to give some instructions. As Kirsten trailed behind the other five towards the farmhouse, she wondered what he was saying. She had a bad feeling. Everything in this operation so far was clinical. She had watched him kill someone he called a dear friend. In her mind, she thought she should have stopped it then, arrested him, but she'd be dead herself. Even now it was going to be difficult.

Maybe she could try and escape, bring the services to wherever here was. One thing she knew was that she couldn't move, couldn't get out until she was aware of what plot they were carrying out. Until she knew what the celebration was, there was no point ducking out. For up to now, she didn't have much. She could talk about an organised death fight they were in. She could nail Darcy for murder, having killed his friend in front of her, but how many of those around her would even speak of that and would even be here to arrest when she got back with reinforcements?

Kirsten traipsed into the farmhouse behind the rest as they made their way towards the shower area. Once again, she simply stripped down, pulled the curtain around her and washed herself. She dried herself behind the shower curtain, quickly stretching out to bring her clothes in, changing, before emerging back to the room beyond the curtain.

She saw a few of the men standing there drying themselves, clearly happy at how they looked, but her mind was swimming. There was an uneasiness running through her. When she had been on the murder teams, it was simple. You found your killer, and you arrested them. When she'd gone to look after that child on Lewis, it was a bit more complicated, but at the end of the day, people were coming for her. Kirsten defended herself.

Now she was stuck in having to act out a role, a role where she was forced to injure people. Quite possibly, they may ask her to kill someone one day, and that would force a conflict on her. How far did you go? How much could you get involved in something like this? This celebration, whatever it was, must be big with the work that was going into it, the numbers of people involved. She was bargaining against life saved in the future, a number she could not know, against those she would protect today.

Kirsten was the first to try to leave the shower room but was told to remain there, so she turned and leaned up against a couple of washbasins in the room. A man in his twenties edged up beside her, looking down on her, for he stood well over six foot. In Kirsten's mind, he reminded her of one of those lifeguard programmes where she could see his rippling chest running into the sea, except she also saw him beating the head off someone, flashing a machete or some other weapon.

'Darcy's right, you can handle yourself. We all just stood and watched.'

'So I saw,' said Kirsten. 'Didn't see anybody coming to help us.'

'Thought you could help yourself, didn't we, boys?' said the man looking across at the others remaining.

A bald man laughed along with him. 'You look rather shapely too. You'd put a bit of a fight up with it, wouldn't you?' The man must only have been a couple of inches taller than Kirsten, though if he had said that in a bar, she felt like she would have gone over and slapped him for it. She saw the tattoos on his arm. She knew better than to underestimate someone just because he didn't look as physically strong as the person next to him.

'I don't think so,' said Kirsten. 'I'm here for a job. Don't try any of that stuff on me.'

'Look, but don't touch, is it?' said the man.

'Can't stop you looking, can I?' said Kirsten. 'But if you touch,

I'll make sure you can't look.'

Behind the bald man, a blond-haired older man of maybe fifty gave out a wolf whistle. 'That's feisty talk,' he said. 'Where'd you learn to fight like that though? A lot of what you do is very clinical, incredibly controlled. You don't have the look of basic military about you.'

'Born fighting on the streets, street-fought in Ireland.' Kirsten was impressed with the Irish brogue she was putting on even at this moment, when inside she was shaking.

The other woman emerged from behind her shower curtain, a towel wrapped around her, and asked Kirsten for her clothes. One of the men stepped over to take them to her, but Kirsten shoved her way in first. 'I don't think so. Here,' she said, throwing the girl the clothes.

The woman was maybe in her thirties, slim and blonde, and had a frame that didn't look fit for fighting, but she certainly knew how to give a lingering eye to the men. Maybe that's how she controlled them. Maybe she didn't have the fists to fight them off in that way. Kirsten made her way back to her sink, resting the edge of her backside on it, staring across the room at the bald man who was leering at her. When the other woman emerged from the shower, she took a position beside Kirsten.

'Sisters together then, is it?' said the bald man. 'I don't mind women together.'

Kirsten felt sick inside, but instead she just held up her hand, indicating that the man would suffer unless he clammed up.

A guard stuck his head into the shower room and told the group to follow him. Kirsten and the other woman led the way and they sat down inside another room with a table and benches on either side. There was water available, as well as soup and bread. Kirsten tore into it, hungry, always aware that she didn't know where the next meal was coming from. One of the men went to talk, but Kirsten raised her hand, indicating she wanted silence. He gave a little laugh, but he complied and the six of them sat together, the only noise being the chewing of food and the occasional splash of the soup.

Then Kirsten heard a dull thud. It was very quiet, but then she heard something like a sack of potatoes hitting the ground. There came another, and another, quickly and in succession. She stood up and walked over towards the window. When she looked out, all she could see was the front driveway and the mountains beyond. Kirsten thought about the orientation of the house. As far as she could gather where they were, she wasn't looking at the rear, looking out where the vans were and where the rectangular ring had been. She heard another thud.

'The man must be doing some digging out there,' said the bald man. 'We'll be lifting up a stash of weapons and that and somebody's going to tell us what we're doing soon. Getting restless now the fun's over.'

Kirsten nearly swore at the word 'fun', but she held her counsel, staring out of the window. Deep inside, she knew nobody was digging anything up. There were no weapons being lifted out of the ground. The first quiet thud she heard and the subsequent thuds in between the lighter ones she thought came from muffled gunfire. In her mind, the louder thud was the bodies hitting the ground. Inside her stomach, she began to feel the bile rise.

She had fought not to kill anyone. She had fought to defend herself to make it look like she was trying, but she was risking all to make sure she would not kill anyone in front of her. Now, this Darcy man had just gone and finished them off. Thirty people had come. No, it was twenty-nine. One hadn't even got here. Maybe they'd had to finish him off somewhere else. Yet those who had come, those who had fought, those who had laid down their lives for Scotland were now going to be in the back of a van with a bullet lodged in them.

Darcy was crazy, Kirsten concluded. Crazy but efficient. It was a level of madness. Some people were just wild, swinging out at anything around them, but not Darcy. Yet, his treatment of human life was so repugnant. He put no value in anyone. Kirsten knew that he put no value in her either. She paced up and down inside the room, noting all the time that the bald man was looking at her. Just to keep him in check, she strode over, staring at him. When his hand came out, she grabbed his wrist, twisting it.

'Okay, girlie. Okay, I get the message.' Kirsten let his hand go. As she continued to pace up and down, she noted that his eyes were still following her.

The door suddenly burst open, and Darcy made his way in. 'Excellent. Replenished. You're going to be doing some training soon, but I need to get you fitted up. I obviously didn't know who was going to make it through, so I need to get you clothing for the job we'll have in hand.'

'What job's that?' asked the bald man.

'Well, you'll find out,' said Darcy, 'but I give nothing away yet. I've got my tailor in to measure you up if that's all right. You,' he said pointing to Kirsten, 'let's get you measured.' Kirsten looked at him and saw the man behind him coming towards her with a tape measure.

'You'll need to strip down for it,' said Darcy, 'just to the underwear. There's no need to get saucy.'

'We can step outside and do it,' said Kirsten.

'No,' said Darcy. 'I want to know my people can hold their own if they have to exploit their sexuality.' Kirsten looked across at the bald-headed man. He was licking his lips at her. Kirsten shook her head, turned her back to those at the benches, took off her top and her trousers, her boots to one side. For three minutes, she stood, arms outstretched while she was measured up. Then she quickly dressed. When she turned around again, the bald-headed man was still looking at her.

'I'll go next,' he said and looked over at Kirsten, 'let you check this out, love.' Kirsten returned to the table, getting herself some more soup and started dipping bread into it, ignoring the antics of the bald man behind her. She could see the shocked face of the other woman and the grins of the other men finding it funny.

When everyone had been measured up, Darcy expressed his satisfaction and turned to them all, saying his tailor would be back in the morning with clothes for everyone.

'Until then,' he said, 'I'm afraid you're going to have to wait in here. In the evening we'll take you back to the bunk beds. Don't ignore the staff,' he said, indicating a couple of his guards. 'They have been instructed to shoot to kill if you go outside of the parameters I've given you. Stay within and you'll be well treated. You will have a TV brought in. There are games, there are magazines, books if you want them. Just relax, ladies and gentlemen, because you've made it. You're going to be Scottish heroes. You're going to show those south of the border just what we're made of. You're going to be the claymore in my hands.'

Kirsten watched the man march out, but the bald-headed

man stood up, turning to the other five. 'That's more like it. We're going to get a crack at the English. I bet you it's a crack at the English.'

'If it suits him,' said the other woman. 'Just be aware if things go wrong, we'll not get out of here.' Kirsten suddenly realised that the woman was astute and maybe understood more about what was going on than this bald-headed man opposite her.

'What do you mean?' he said.

'What I mean is we're expendable. Don't be surprised that what he tells us to do ends up being a suicide mission.'

'I've fought enough of those,' said the man. 'One day your bullet comes. You don't worry about it. You just get on with it, and if I die going out taking down some of the English, it'll be a pleasure.' Kirsten scanned the faces of the others and she wasn't so sure that they were as patriotic.

Chapter 16

The next day, the new clothing arrived as promised. The group were woken up, having slept in one of the dorms, at 7:00 a.m., with Darcy marching in with a small number of his guards. They quickly took away all bunks except for three doubles and then put up some temporary wardrobes. A range of clothing was put into each, and Darcy asked that the group try them all to make sure that they fitted correctly.

Kirsten looked at what was provided for her. She smiled when she saw the black cargo trousers, t-shirt, black jumper. There was even a balaclava. She saw them as clothes she'd be comfortable in, but she also saw the crop top, the short skirt, the high heels. Not every outfit was like that. Just one particular one. There was also a smart suit to wear as well as a rather stained and frumpy jumper and jeans.

'It's all just different looks,' said Darcy when he saw Kirsten, looking at the skirt she'd been given. It was one of the ones that her mother would've complained about if she'd gone out wearing it back when she was a teen, back before she'd lost her.

'Don't worry,' said Darcy. 'I've got different looks. I'm

not interested in you in that way, but you may have to wear something like that. You may have to use your sexuality. The men have a similar outfit they may need to wear.'

'I think I'll be happier in the black,' said Kirsten.

'I think you would, but this is no way to talk to each other. So far you have a name for me, Mr Darcy. I'm going to give out names to the rest of you because we can't talk like this forever. We have some preparation time to achieve our ends. First of all, you over there,' he said pointing at the large man with the dark hair. 'That's Mr Harris, beside him with no hair is Mr Donovan, Mr Bingley over there, along with Mr Wickham, and you,' he said pointing at the other woman, 'Miss Musgrove. As for our more-happily-clad-in-black friend,' he said looking at Kirsten, 'you shall be Miss Nash.

'Please remember these names, only use these names. Do not use your first name, do not use your surname. Only these names. If you use your name or talk about your background in any detail such as you can be identified from it, you'll be removed from the team.'

There was a silence left after the words and Kirsten understood what it meant. You'd be going home in a van, except you wouldn't be breathing when you did.

'I have to be totally strict about this,' said Darcy. 'We need to have secrecy within our group. If something goes wrong, we must not be able to rat on each other. I don't trust people. We can all give out information. If we don't have it, it can never be passed on.'

'That's a wise precaution,' said the bald man.

'Indeed, it is, Mr Donovan,' said Darcy. 'We've got work to do this afternoon. I want you outside in half an hour, probably best you wear the combat fatigues. I think Miss Nash is going to enjoy this one.' Darcy smiled at Kirsten, and she was quite unsure how to take him. He swept out the door, his guards following him.

'He seems to have a thing for you, Nash,' said Miss Musgrove.

'Seems to have a thing for both of us. Have you seen some of these outfits?' said Kirsten.

'He doesn't have anything for anybody,' said Harris, the large man. 'He's just getting us to play roles. That's all he wants, us to play a role. You'll find out soon enough when it's going to be and what it's going to be.'

'You've done stuff like this before, haven't you?' asked Musgrove.

'Hey,' said Bingley and Kirsten realised she hadn't really heard him speak before. The man was just under six foot with mousey-brown hair. He was muscly, if not stocky. 'We don't talk about the past, remember? I think if he found out any of us were blagging about operations we've done and places we've been, we won't be here. Kindly don't ask and don't tell me.'

'That's a good idea,' said Kirsten. 'I think that's something we all need to hold to.' *Especially as I am a former police detective and now, I spy*, she thought. *I really don't need my past coming up.*

Kirsten quickly took her black clothing and changed into the fatigues before lying down on her bed. Twenty minutes later, Darcy arrived with his guards again, and they were taken outside. Kirsten saw that behind the farmhouse there was a long track. It seemed to have several potholes in it, the surface being extremely rough. It was gravel and to either side was boggy moorland. She wondered at the car that was waiting for them. It looked like quite a souped-up version of a saloon car, but along the roof were a couple of handrails and down beneath the doors she could see a foot rail.

'Where we're going to go,' said Darcy, 'I'm going to need someone who can operate when the situation is bad. There's going to be a lot of air rushing past and I need someone who can move along in it, but we'll start today with the basics. All you've got to do, stand on the side of the car and hang on.'

'What?' blurted Miss Musgrove. 'You can't be serious.'

'No, you can't,' said Donovan. 'She'll not hang on for two minutes. She'll be off in an instant.'

'You're going to run us over those bumps,' said Kirsten. 'We'll get thrown here, there, and everywhere.'

'Now, now, team,' said, Mr Darcy, 'I expect a bit more effort than that. Up to it, I'll be driving the car.'

Kirsten made her way over to the car behind Darcy. He slipped into the driver's seat. She stood at the front, her feet on the rail below, her hands holding tight. She leaned back off the car. The others took their place, two beside her and three on the other side. Directly beside Kirsten was Miss Musgrove, who looked extremely worried. The men on the other side were not looking particularly chuffed either. 'If you fall off, Nash,' said Donovan, 'don't worry, I'll jump down and save you. I'll get on top of you.'

Kirsten absolutely wanted to smash the man's face in. All through the day he kept looking at her, but she had to hold it in check, the last thing she needed was a fight kicking off. She couldn't be taken away; there were too many lives at stake—and her own—if she somehow fouled this up.

'Just hang on,' said Kirsten, 'or you can watch me from the moorland.'

Darcy started the car up, and at first, he drove at a steady thirty mile an hour. The car bumped here and there, Kirsten hanging on tight. They'd only gone one hundred metres when Musgrove fell off, rolling into the moorland. Kirsten lifted her hand off, ready to jump down to help, but the car sped up.

'Like he's going to wait for her,' said Donovan, and he started to move his way up towards Kirsten. The track became more winding, and as they hit a large pothole Kirsten felt her feet lift and they slid off the foot rail touching the ground, but she held onto the top rail and pulled herself back up. Donovan was hanging on with one arm, and brought himself back up, but as Kirsten looked across the car, two of the men had fallen off. Strong Mr Harris grinned at her.

As the car swung this way and that, Kirsten hung on for grim death. The car turned this way and that, and across from her, she saw the smile on Harris's face suddenly go as his hand slipped. His foot caught the ground and he disappeared off into the moorland, just as the car turned onto a tarmac piece of road. Unlike the gravel path, it was smooth, but it still cut through the moorland and Kirsten heard the car begin to roar. Previously, they would have been lucky if they had managed forty miles an hour turning around the corners that were sharp, but now here on the tarmac road, Darcy opened up the throttle.

Kirsten wrapped her arms inside the metal fixture at the top of the car, hanging on tight. Her hair blew out behind her, and as she turned, she saw Donovan making his way up along the rail towards her. He was no less than an arm's distance away, but he was also hanging on tight.

'You're not going to show me up on this one,' he shouted at Kirsten. 'I'm taking you out.' He began to punch hard down on her nearest arm. She almost slipped and Donovan moved forward, reaching up with his hand, grabbing her by the hair. He started yanking her head backwards, trying to pull her off the car.

'What the hell are you doing?' yelled Kirsten. The car picked up in speed, and she swore it must be going over seventy miles an hour by now. She felt her arm beginning to slip. Kirsten realised that if she didn't act quickly, her grip would go, and she'd fall. At this speed she couldn't guarantee what would happen then.

Leaning out backwards and holding on with her hand, she couldn't get the strength to pull herself back up, so she did the only move she thought she could. She stamped hard down on Donovan's foot. Briefly, his hold on her hair was released. She pulled herself up towards the car, putting her right hand on the top rail. She spun, letting her left arm trail out, her elbow ahead of her. She caught Donovan in the head, and she saw his hands begin to slip.

Keeping her right hand on the fixture, she grabbed him just underneath his throat, pulling him towards her as both of his hands left the rail. The man was about to fall. Every instinct of Kirsten was to keep him here, safe up on the car, despite how obnoxious and pervy he had been, but as she did so, he reached up, grabbing her in the stomach and then threw a punch directly into it. Kirsten doubled slightly, but she'd taken punches like that before in her time. She reached forward with her hand, pulling them closer. With the wind pulling at them, she nutted him in the forehead. She released her grip and watched as Donovan fell off the car. His legs hit the tarmac, but his body then spun, and he fell off into the moorland below.

Darcy brought the car to a halt shortly afterwards, but Kirsten remained on it holding tight to the railing at the top of the car.

'Well done, Miss Nash, I think you can come off now. It seems you've managed to hang on better than all of them. I thought you might stay on the track, but when the speed got up, I thought everyone was bound to go.'

Kirsten looked at Darcy like he was some sort of madman. 'Donovan tried to pull me off; he tried to take me down,' said Kirsten.

'He is a spirited fellow, isn't he? If he's still alive, he's a good addition to the team.'

Kirsten nearly swore, but instead she stepped down off the car and looked back down the track, 'If he's alive, I've failed in what I was trying to do,' she said. Although she didn't mean it, she put the best of her voice into it.

'Good,' said Darcy. 'I like a little bit of fire in my people.'

It was half an hour later, and Kirsten was sitting in the day room, as they'd started to call it. It was where they'd had their meal before. There was a TV in the corner, plenty of papers around, as well as some other magazines. Darcy had provided all sorts, ranging from glamorous homes to an array of pornographic material. He said as they would be there for a while, he wanted to make sure everyone was catered for.

Kirsten was watching the television, and she could see the scenes across Scotland were getting worse. Vandalism, knives, fighting breaking out at marches, both sides of the debate clashing with each other, the police caught in the middle, as ever. Macleod's face came on the television, again saying they had nothing in the hunt for the murderer of MSP Macritchie.

Donovan had been taken away to be looked at, but Kirsten reckoned he was not going to hospital. There'll be somebody here. One of those backstreet surgeons that got employed. She was not surprised when Donovan limped in, snarling at her, before he sat down in the corner. Darcy was following.

'Well, well, I knew our women were good, but I didn't know this one was that good. We'll have exercises for the next couple of weeks, I'll be able to say a bit more about what we're going to do by then. We'll also be getting a lecture. Have any of you had any use of explosives before in your life?'

Harris, Donovan and Bingley held up their hands. 'Good. You other three are going to have to learn how to set triggers, how to make things go boom.'

'What's our target then?' said Harris. 'This better be good. We're putting a lot of work into this.'

'Oh, it'll be the best. It'll be the best.' Darcy looked at the TV. 'Fourteen days,' he said. 'Fourteen days till the referendum vote. You won't be here more than two weeks, ladies and gentlemen. Two weeks, and then it will be the great celebration.'

Kirsten shuddered as she looked at Darcy. There was a twinkle in his eye, and the grin was almost childish. *He's actually enjoying this*, she thought. *Who knows what he's got lined up next.*

Chapter 17

Kirsten let the last ripples of water flow across her before giving her body a shake. She reached a hand out to the floor beyond the shower curtain, picked up the towel, and began to dry herself. Once outside, she veered away from the shower area to the room with the bunks and saw that no one was there. Quickly, she got on her underwear and changed into the black outfit that she'd been wearing for most of the last week. Every night it had been taken away and washed and brought back the next morning as the training had continued.

There were timed exercises, training in hand-to-hand combat. Darcy also insisted on teaching them how to use their voice to control people, calm them down. Kirsten got the idea that they'd be taking over a live target, something with people where they'd have to intercept it. Timing was of the essence to Darcy and several times they practiced jumping onto the side of moving cars. The car was once again fitted with the railings and by now they were getting quite expert at it, albeit, the car never seemed to go above thirty miles an hour. The initial test had obviously been for something different.

Kirsten heard the door open, and Donovan walked in with

a half limp, one caused when he fell off the car. He kept telling Kirsten that his knee didn't feel right, but she ignored every protest he made. The guy came after her and tried to throw her off. If she wasn't so keen about not making a ruckus, she'd have planted him one by now, beat him back off properly, but she wasn't too sure how Darcy would react to that. Donovan seemed to have expertise with explosives that Darcy needed, so she needed to tread a fine line. After all, the only thing she was bringing to the party was some dangerous fists and possibly an ability to hang on.

'I see I missed you in the shower again. Pity, you really must give me a heads-up next time.'

'You come anywhere near that shower when I'm in it,' said Kirsten, 'and they'll be washing your blood out of the sinks.'

The man stared back at her. At first, Kirsten kept the grimace she had. It helped that she threw in the touch of the Irish accent because that always seemed to unnerve people. The friendliest nation on the planet until you heard them talk in that mildly threatening way. It was funny how an accent could be jovial but sinister at the same time.

'Anyway, Darcy wants us in.'

'Now?' asked Kirsten.

'You, me, and Harris, not the others. Says he needs to talk to us.'

Kirsten felt unsure about what was being asked. Had something been discovered? Was she being brought in? Was Darcy looking to seek to solve the problem between Donovan and herself? There was nothing for it but to go anyway. Kirsten shook her shoulders and put on the jacket that hung at her wardrobe.

'Maybe he wants to watch me kick your face in,' said Kirsten.

'But I reckon he's giving Harris a go first just so you don't bleed too badly.' Donavan made a move towards her, but Kirsten reached out with her hands, slapping his out of the way. 'Just give me an excuse, Donovan. Any excuse.'

Kirsten let him leave the room first, following him along to a room she hadn't been in yet. It was small with a single table in the middle and Darcy was already sitting by it.

'Good to see you again, Miss Nash, looking so well freshened up. You, me and the boys are going to go for a little trip, so sit down, shut up, and listen. I'll tell you what we're doing.'

Kirsten took a seat opposite Darcy with Harris on her left, Donovan on her right. She sat back at the table, but Harris was up on his elbows, all ears.

'This is it, Darcy. Are we going for it?'

'No,' said Darcy. 'We just need to collect some items, but I want you with me in case there's trouble. We'll be going to a house in the middle of nowhere. We'll get there first, and some gentlemen will be coming along to drop off our items. If I give the word, you're to stop them. They may try and leave with things that they shouldn't.'

'How many of them will there be?' asked Kirsten.

'I'm only expecting the two,' said Darcy. 'One who's doing the deal with me and a bit of muscle with him, but there may be people outside the house. That's why you're going to be hidden, Nash.' Kirsten nodded. It made sense for she didn't look threatening or intimidating. He could have Harris for that and Donovan, too. Although, if they were looking at explosives, Donovan might be there to check them over.

'You're going to make sure the goods are good, Donovan, and Harris, you're my protection. Anything looks out of order you step in. Understood?'

'Yes, Mr Darcy,' said Harris, almost pleased with himself.

'But this will go smoothly,' Darcy said. 'Okay, so nobody jumps the gun on it. We'll be in the house. Nash is outside. They'll bring the goods in. Donovan here will look at them. I'll brief him by then on what they are, what they need to do. He'll check that they're the right thing, and then we'll give some money to our friends, and they will disappear off.'

'Will they be armed?' asked Kirsten.

'Why do you ask that?' said Darcy.

'Your guys were armed here when we were having our little fight out in the rectangle. They're still armed when they walk around. It seems there's not a lot of trust going on. Maybe their trust will be based on bringing guns with them.'

'I don't know if they'll be armed.'

'Should I carry a firearm then?' asked Kirsten.

'Miss Nash, have you ever used a firearm?'

'No,' said Kirsten, aware the street fighter was unlikely to have held one.

'Well, then I'm not going to put a loaded weapon into a client's hand, am I? You've got your weapons on the end of your arms and you know how to use them. You will use them if I say so.'

'Yes, Mr Darcy,' said Kirsten. She'd learned over the last week that the best way to get on his side was to simply give straightforward answers.

'Good,' said Darcy and he swept a hand through his blond hair. 'Eyes and ears. Picked you three because you seem the more sensible. Well, except for Donovan here. I've picked him because he knows his explosives. He doesn't seem to have an ounce of sense on him,' said Darcy, laughing. Donovan looked at him as if he'd been hurt.

'Well, you ought to quit sniffing over Miss Nash because you want to get it on. Are you trying to provoke her into hitting you? She will. She kicked your arse off that car. She'll plant you here. Don't underestimate Miss Nash and don't give me any frigging problems.' With that, Darcy slammed his fist in the table in front of Donovan. 'Because if you do, you won't be around here for long. Do you understand me?'

'Yes, Mr. Darcy, of course.' Donovan flashed his eyes towards Kirsten.

'And don't look at her. She's not the problem. You are.'

Well, at least I'm not in the firing line, thought Kirsten. *Maybe I'll keep him off my back or I'll just keep what he's doing to our quieter moments.'*

Darcy led the three of them outside and advised he would be taking Harris aside for a moment before showing the van to Kirsten and Donovan. Once they sat down, blindfolds were put over their eyes and Kirsten heard the door shut.

'Don't think that I'm finished with you, lassie,' said Donovan.

'You heard him,' said Kirsten. 'Don't come for me because I won't give him anything to finish you off with. You'll just be a mess. I know how to hurt.'

The door of the van opened again, and Kirsten heard somebody else get in before the door was shut. About twenty seconds later, the van drove away, but she reckoned that Darcy must have been in the front seat doing the driving. She sat back, tried to breathe normally, and relax into the evening. This shouldn't come to anything. It should be straightforward. It's just a drop-off, so all she had to do was try to identify as many people as she could, bring them to mind, and work out what they were handing over.

Kirsten wasn't sure when she knew all this how to get a

message out, but at the moment she knew so little. It wasn't worth the risk of trying to break away. The whole operation could go underground, and she didn't have enough to be able to follow it. About an hour later, the van came to a halt and Kirsten heard someone walking around the outside. The door opened and Darcy advised they could take their blindfolds off. Outside the light was thinning, the end of the day approaching. Kirsten jumped out of the van to look around.

'You've got a perimeter here,' he said. 'You've got fifteen minutes to scan it. Then I want you back here at the house.'

'Do you not trust me?' said Kirsten.

'No, I don't,' said Darcy. 'You trust no one in this operation.'

'Sometimes you have to trust,' said Kirsten. 'Miss Musgrove trusted me when were in that rectangle fighting for our lives.'

'I'm not Miss Musgrove and I don't need to trust my life to anyone. You've got fourteen minutes. Get a move on.'

Kirsten disappeared off into the forest that surrounded the ruined house. There was only one road up to it. When she sprinted further, she could see a main road some distance away. She reckoned it would take her at least ten minutes to get there and ten minutes to get back. Darcy wasn't stupid. He looked after every flight risk, every problem that there was, so Kirsten did her job and scouted where the surroundings were, possible areas where they could drop off extra people. Fourteen minutes later, she was back, talking to Darcy.

'What have you found?' he said.

'There's a couple of pinch points as you come up the road. They could duck out without you seeing them, move their way up through undergrowth. Mainly on the west side; that's where I'd see them coming.'

'And you gleaned all that after being a street fighter,' said

Darcy.

'We're not to talk about our pasts,' said Kirsten. 'I've done other things, but I'm not going to say what they are.'

'Good,' said Darcy. 'You're learning. I think you're going to be most useful to me, Miss Nash. You've got a half an hour, then they'll be here. I want you sat outside this front door for the next twenty minutes, then go and disappear. Keep an eye on our guests as they arrive.'

Darcy turned around and walked into the house. The roof had caved in and the interior of the house was a mess, but someone had cleared a central area and there was a pop-up table sitting there. Donovan was sitting on his backside on the ground, his job not having started yet, but Harris was walking beside Darcy, on his shoulder, watching everyone closely.

After twenty minutes, Kirsten disappeared into the night but found herself sitting beside a tree, watching headlights appear on the road that led up to the house. She saw the vehicle stop and someone got out roughly where she thought they would. She made her way down and watched from a distance until she saw a black figure start to move up towards the house. Kirsten kept a distance, realising the undergrowth still made a noise when you moved through it, but fortunately, the wind was enough tonight that any minor sounds were getting eaten up. The figure she was following was a man, for the shoulders were broad. He had that stocky build of a man, but he moved clumsily, and Kirsten could see hanging from his shoulder was a weapon. It was a brutal one, a handheld machine gun, but she realised that the accuracy of it would be limited because she knew that brand was hard to hold. They kicked like hell—really were quite indiscriminate weapons.

Despite this, she watched him as he got closer to the house, bent down, and fixed his gun on what was going on inside, Kirsten cast a glance inside and saw lights shining down on the central table. A couple of bags were left on the table and Donovan was inside them, examining. He seemed to be taking his time and Darcy was getting impatient.

'Is it the right stuff?' he said.

'As far as I can tell,' said Donovan. 'I'm just checking through the timer. I can't open this too quickly. It could go off.'

'Just get it done,' said Darcy, ''til we get out of here.'

Kirsten realised that for all Darcy knew, she could've gone at this point. He had to trust her if he was going to have someone on watch. While it didn't feel that he was totally sold on her, it did indicate that she wasn't at least a suspect, someone there to infiltrate his organisation. After a moment, Donovan stepped back, turned to Darcy, and gave a nod.

'The money,' said a voice from inside. It must have been the Arab men who'd come to do business, but Kirsten couldn't see them from where she was. She did note that the man outside with the machine gun had raised it slightly.

'There is no money,' said Darcy. 'There is nothing. Just leave. You don't need paid. I'm giving you your life.'

There was a commotion inside. Kirsten got closer to the man with the machine gun, sneaking up behind him. From where he was, he could see right inside the house. As she got close to him, she noticed he was watching one of the Arab men inside. A hand was raised and then dropped as if signalling for something, but nothing came. Instead, the man with the machine gun was lying face down in the undergrowth, out cold. Kirsten had seen the signal and disabled him before he had a chance to react. She saw the Arab man inside panic, turn to look outside, and then she heard Darcy questioning him.

'What? Did you bring extras? Were you just going to take our money?'

They'd come to do business, thought Kirsten. *They'd brought it in good faith. Donovan said it was there. The only person that has broken this deal was Darcy. He didn't bring any money.*

'Go,' said Darcy. 'Go.' The Arab man looked at him, turned and pushed open the door, and began to run out of the house. Kirsten kept herself hidden away, confident that Darcy had told the men to go, but then she saw him turn to Harris and give a nod. Harris stepped forward to the door of the house, and in his hand, Kirsten could see a handgun. Her instinct inside was to shout to the Arab men, to scream for them to get away, but if she did that her cover would be blown. She'd have to run for her life. There'd be nothing known about the organisation and what they were going to do. Instead, Kirsten watched in fascinated horror as Harris first shot one man in the back, and then another. He then calmly walked out, standing over them to finish them off.

'Miss Nash,' said Darcy. 'Where are you?'

Kirsten stood up. 'Here, Darcy.'

'Did they bring others?'

'He's out cold at my feet.'

'Mr Harris,' said Darcy. 'Finish him off.'

Kirsten stood in horror as Harris walked past her and fired two close shots into the man. She had looked after him, she had cared for him, but still they'd finished him off, and by the looks of it, Darcy wasn't finished yet.

Chapter 18

'Miss Nash,' said Darcy, 'Kindly take care of the bodies and put them in the van. We'll head somewhere else to get rid of them.' Kirsten looked at Darcy who stared back, impatient at her lack of motion. 'Get a move on; we can't sit around here all night. Give her a hand, Harris. Donavan, get those explosives into the van.'

Harris came along, bent down picking up one of the bodies by the feet, and Kirsten grabbed the arms. They made their way over to the van, dumping him inside. She went back twice more with Harris, and the man seemed to grin as he threw the Arabs into the van. Kirsten had seen some grim sights in her time, but this was striking at her core.

Once all three bodies were inside the van, Kirsten was instructed to sit back in her seat. Her feet were touching a body and she felt herself shiver as she sat in the seat, allowing Darcy to put a blindfold over her eyes again. As the van pulled away, she could feel her feet being pushed this way and that. A sigh came out of the man at her feet, the last wind escaping, and Kirsten nearly jumped. She'd seen this all before, and it was a fond trick of the forensic department to take the new officers inside and let them see the surreal. She remembered a colleague standing beside her collapsing at that point, fainting.

She reckoned they were in the van for about an hour before it stopped again and she heard the door slide open. In the near distance, she could hear waves, the crashing sea, and she stepped out into a breezy night. It was overcast, but as she looked out, she could see lights from boats far off in the distance. When her eyes had adjusted, she was able to make out the edge of a cliff.

'Donovan, Harris, take those explosives out over to the side here. I want to check through them all.'

'But I looked at them,' said Donovan. 'I looked at them back in the ruined house.'

'You did, but I didn't. I want to see that everything's in place. We can't screw this up. You, Nash, get these bodies over the cliff. I think you're strong enough to do that, aren't you?'

Kirsten nodded and returned to the van, pulling one of the bodies out by the feet. She dragged it to the edge, not looking at the face. She'd found that with people before, faces came back to haunt you, but if you could focus on their chest, their legs, the hips, the arms, something else, it never hit you as bad.

It took Kirsten five minutes to bring the three bodies over to the cliff edge. As she was about to throw them, she reached up, pulled at her hair hard. A small number of strands came out, and she reached down stuffing them into one of the Arab's mouths. She reached up and grabbed another few strands of hair putting into the next mouth, and then the last. She then went, grabbed the first body and saying a prayer, she pushed it off the cliff edge. She did the same with the second, not stopping to look to see the state of the body as they crashed down onto the rocks below.

When she got to the third, her courage was up and Kirsten suddenly had an idea. It could work. She whipped off the shoes of the Arab, and after pushing him off the edge, she moved them to sit just behind a large tuft of grass. From the van, you would struggle to see them, and Kirsten reckoned that Darcy wouldn't come nearer, he was too busy with the explosives. She made her way back to the van, sat on the edge of it, waiting for them to come back. They were just a short distance away but utterly engrossed in the explosives. She saw Darcy take care lifting each packet. Maybe he was thinking about how they would be planted, how they would be carried. Maybe Kirsten would be charged with taking them in.

It was as she was waiting, Kirsten saw the newspaper lying in the van floor. She picked it up, opened it, and started looking at the violence that was erupting throughout the nation. Here and there were skirmishes, people throwing punches and then doing worse, time and again. The murder of Angus Macritchie and then the attempted murder of Jennifer Galson, who were used as excuses to attack those who were more nationalist bent.

As Kirsten read, she thought the unionist side were as bad as the nationalist, and she just wanted the whole thing to end. The question always seemed to divide her country, always seemed to rip it apart. She remembered last time seeing neighbours at each other's throats, but last time it was simply signs that were torn down. None of the politicians had been attacked and Darcy, he was somebody even madder.

Then Kirsten had an idea. She looked across at Darcy, still with his head down engaged in what he was doing. She leaned back so her legs just sat outside the van, but her body was inside. Taking the centre page of the newspaper, she took it out and left the paper on the floor. Carefully, she pulled an article apart so there was only it left. Taking off one of her shoes, she took the lace on the edge of it, and carefully began to poke through several words within the article. It was slow work. She kept leaning out time and again to see if Darcy was looking, but he kept away from her, and Kirsten completed her task.

The message Kirsten spelt out simply said, 'Attack English on the night of the referendum.' She wanted to put the word celebration in, but she had neither time nor the room within the article. She folded up the paper in her hand, and after putting her shoe back on, slowly walked over to the edge, looking down from the cliff. With her left hand, she reached into the shoe behind the tuft of grass, dropping the message into it. Once the message was inside, Kirsten looked once more over the edge and saw one of the bodies being taken away into the water, the other two having previously disappeared.

'Aren't you done yet? I thought you were back at the van,' said Darcy.

'I'm not used to this work,' said Kirsten. She grasped her stomach, gagging hard before managing to throw up over the edge of the cliff.

'I thought you had a stronger stomach than that.'

Kirsten got to her feet, turned around and squared up to the man, 'The job's done, isn't it? Who cares if I throw a bit of sick over the edge?'

Darcy made his move, got to the edge and looked down. He could feel the rain beginning to fall from the sky. 'It'll be washed away. It won't be a problem,' he said. 'Next time think about that. You don't go going sick over where you just dropped a load of bodies. You'll leave DNA.'

'Of course,' said Kirsten. 'Sorry,' and she hung her head as if in shame. She noted Darcy looking at her, shaking his own head and making his way back to the van. What he didn't realise was that she was standing directly between him and the shoes behind the tuft of grass.

'It's time to get going, time to get in the van. Come on.' With that, he made his move, ushering Kirsten and the other two men into the van, blindfolding them once more before driving off. Kirsten swung her feet out as he did so, happy that nothing was blocking them anymore. But she also heard the rain bouncing off the roof and hoped that the message inside the shoes wouldn't become so wet that it would be destroyed.

* * *

Seoras Macleod sat in a seat in his office and was fed up. He had been following a lost cause for the last few weeks and had to go onto television to say that leads had gone cold. Yes, they had two people who attempted the murder of Galson, but so far, there was no one attached to Angus Macritchie. Of course, there was nothing he could move on without jeopardising Kirsten in her work, but as it was, he didn't have any information despite his team searching long and hard into the records of a few dodgy men they'd picked up.

He walked to the edge of his office, opened the door, and looked out into the room that housed the rest of his team. Hope McGrath, the redheaded six-foot sergeant, looked back at him, her eyes looking tired, and her shoulders drooped. Beside her, Alan Ross, a detective constable, was working away on the computer, diligent as ever, while across from him, his newest recruit, Clarissa Urquhart, the older sergeant, flamboyant, eccentric, but as tough as they came, also looked despondent.

'I take it we have nothing else then?' he asked.

'No, Seoras. Nothing's come through and the last lead we ran through was a dead end. Clarissa has been on that all day and it came to nothing. We need a break, we need something to fold. Did you see the latest news report, Seoras?'

'No. Was working through the reports to sign them off. Why? What's up?'

'Down in Glasgow, man in intensive care tried to stop somebody ripping down his unionist sign. A scuffle broke out. Somebody smashed his head in with a large stone.'

'This is getting crazy,' said Macleod. 'Whatever happened to this country? Why can't we be civilised? We had a civilised country once.'

'No, we didn't,' said Hope. 'When have we ever been civilised? We fought against ourselves, with ourselves, with everybody else. Last time we joined the union, they had to pay us. Typical our country goes into something because you get paid.'

'One that needed the money,' said Urquhart.

'I thought we were getting more progressive,' said Ross, 'with the freedoms that my kind now enjoy.'

'I thought so too,' said Macleod, 'but there you go, but remember, nose to the grindstone. We're not doing this simply for ourselves.'

'Have you heard anything from her?' asked Hope. Kirsten Stewart had worked with Hope McGrath, Alan Ross, and Detective Inspector Macleod, and the team had a fondness for her. They were aware of the path she had taken and now, she seemed to speak to them so rarely.

'I've heard nothing,' said Macleod. 'It's all silent. I contacted that boss of hers, but she's saying nothing and trying to get a hold of her was a nightmare anyway. It sounds like she's talking to everybody, all the politicians. First minister, leader of Opposition, everyone wants a handle on this.'

'They're probably scared,' said Ross. 'After all, they've come for the politicians, even those on the National side, probably wondering if somebody's going to have a pot shot back.'

'That's not what we need,' said Macleod. 'If that happens, it doesn't take long before we are in freefall, before things really deteriorate.'

'Uniform said it's rough out there at the moment, a lot of tension. There's a lot of tension in the station,' said Clarissa. 'I was downstairs having to separate two of the PCs. All about who owned the oil, where the money would go, who would have it right or wrong? Then what will we be called? The Scottish National Police Force, one was saying.'

'Did they mention the Queen?' asked Ross. Clarissa shook her head. 'I was down earlier, and someone was talking about the Queen and that really kicked off some tension. Two of them nearly came to blows.'

'This is the station. We're the police. We're meant to keep order, not kick off a riot,' said Macleod. 'If I go down there, I'll break them, I'll hold them up and kick them in the backside out of here.'

'I think in today's language, you're going to reprimand them, sir,' said Hope, half-smiling.

'No, I won't. I'll kick their backside out of here. We're the police, we stand for something. We have to do things the right way. There's others to sort things out in that fashion.' Macleod's face suddenly fell down somewhat and his eyes didn't look up at the team.

'You mean Kirsten, don't you?' said Hope. 'Has she gone in? Is she like undercover?'

'I don't get told those things,' said Macleod. 'I'm lucky I get told anything.' He closed the door but noted that Clarissa Urquhart had picked up the phone. As he sat back down in the seat, he saw the door open to his office and Hope poked her head in.

'Well, we've got something else on the go,' she said. 'Got a call from a walker. I mean, it's really late.'

Macleod looked over and saw the clock on the wall said 4:00 a.m. 'Who'd go walking at this time?' he asked.

'I don't know if a walker or somebody who's had too much, but they found some shoes, sir. Found them at the edge of a cliff.'

'Okay,' said Macleod. 'Has he told the Coastguard. It's not really for us, is it?'

'They called the Coastguard, Seoras, but the Coastguard called us. It appears they found a piece of paper in one of the shoes. It was a newspaper from yesterday. The officer there said that certain words have been punched out. He thought it might have been coded.'

Macleod flew from his seat, racing towards his coat. 'Get everyone,' he said. 'Everyone now, we go straight there. Tell the Coastguard to take it easy. I don't want a lot of noise. I don't want a lot of activity. Until I get there, we keep this as quiet as possible.'

'What's the matter, Seoras? It's not like we haven't found a pair of shoes before. It's a newspaper with some holes punched in it.'

'Think about it, Hope,' said Macleod. 'If you're in the dark somewhere, if you're in and you can't get a message out, how do you do it?'

'But this could just be some bit of paper, somebody mucking

about.'

'It could, but I haven't heard anything. Nobody's told me anything, and if this is her calling, we need to keep it quiet or she's going to be in real trouble.'

Chapter 19

Detective Inspector Seoras Macleod stood at the cliff edge looking out into the morning sea. The orange lifeboat was going backwards and forwards across the water. It had already picked up one body and brought it back to the crime scene. The forensic van had taken the body inside, shortly to make its way back to the station for further analysis. The morning was cool although the sky was bright and the cliff edge well north of Inverness seemed the perfect place to be, if not for the dark reason why he was there. The sea with its rolling breakers of white made a perfect vista.

They found the pair of shoes sitting behind a large tuft of grass and inside was a piece of paper. Macleod had looked at the message, or so he thought, for there were specific words punched out. Ross was currently seeking a copy of the paper so that the code could be deciphered.

'Detective Inspector,' a voice came from behind him, but he knew who it was already, the voice having been a daily part of work life in recent years. Jona Nakamura, the lead forensic officer at Inverness Station, was making her way towards him. 'Inspector, I think I've got something you want to know.'

'What's that?' asked Macleod.

'There's some hair in the mouth of our body, not just a fine strand, but a reasonable amount of it, and it's not embedded in the teeth, it's stuck in under the tongue. Firstly, when we found him, he'd already washed up along the rocks. His mouth doesn't seem to have been contaminated heavily with the seawater.'

'He's got hair in his mouth?' said Macleod. 'Maybe he had a fight before he went over, maybe he bit into someone.'

'No, Inspector, you don't seem to understand, I think I recognise the hair.'

'You recognise the hair?' queried Macleod, 'I know you're good, Jona, but recognising hair? How does hair look different? You've got various different colours, but outside of that.'

'I would say that this hair colour would be a match for a former detective constable of yours.'

'You think it's Kirsten's? Are you sure?'

'Of course, I'm not sure, Inspector. I'm going back to the lab. We've got her DNA on file. I'll know shortly, but I thought you'd want to know straight away.'

'Indeed, I do,' said Macleod. After thanking the forensic officer, he made a beeline for Hope McGrath, his sergeant.

'Close this site down immediately, I need to get the cox on that lifeboat, I need to talk to the coastguard. We need to make this an exercise.'

'Make it an exercise? I don't understand, Seoras.'

'Jona believes she may have found Kirsten's hair in the mouth of the dead body. I think this is a message. We've also got the note in the shoe with the punched-out holes. If she has been here and if she has been involved in the bodies, we can't have them seeing that there's a major police operation here. We can't have them seeing that bodies have been found. If she's sending us a message, it needs to come in quietly and without anyone noticing.'

'I got you, Seoras, I'm on it.'

Two minutes later, a phone was thrust into Macleod's hand, and he began speaking to the local coastguard. Shortly after that was the launch operations manager of the local lifeboat station, and the RNLI headquarters in the south. Within an hour, there was a minimal presence on scene, but the lifeboat continued to pass to and fro in the sea, but now apparently on exercise, according to its Facebook page. Macleod had moved away in the car, a good half a mile wondering where to position himself exactly. He didn't want to be too far away in case the lifeboat found another body, but on the other hand, he didn't want to put more people where the body was found than he had to.

'Not easy waiting, is it?' said Hope McGrath.

'Where's Ross with that blessed newspaper? Hasn't he found one yet? It can't be that difficult to pick up a copy.'

'I believe he's decoding it for you, sir.'

'Tell him not to. Tell him no. The more I think about it, no. Tell him I want him to work on the body we found. It was an Arab gentleman, so find out who he is and where he came from, but keep it quiet. Ross only, keep it within the four of us in the team.'

'Do you really think she sent this message through?'

'She's resourceful, Kirsten,' said Macleod. 'She always was different, able to think like that.'

'Able to think like you, you mean?' said Hope. 'Sometimes I thought the two of you were thick as thieves.'

Macleod raised his eyebrow, 'And you kept that quiet, didn't you? She was born to that life, though. She's clever, thinks on her feet, can truly handle herself.'

'You do miss her, don't you?'

'Of course, I do,' said Macleod, 'I was fond of Kirsten, very fond of her. I hope she's okay.' With that, his mobile phone rang and Macleod pressed the button to answer the call.

'Inspector, it's Jona here. I can confirm that the hair we found inside the body of the Arab gentleman is indeed that of Kirsten Stewart.'

'That doesn't go anywhere else,' said Macleod. 'You bury it. You don't show that information to anyone, you don't put the result on file. Do you understand me?' said Macleod.

'That's not very standard practice.'

'This is not a very standard operation. I need to go and speak to someone, Jona, someone who really will know what to do with this. In the meantime, see what help you can give Ross with identifying our Arab gentleman, but keep it low, I don't want anyone finding out.

* * *

Loch Ness rippled due to a prevailing wind that was sweeping across it towards Macleod. He told no one he was leaving the office. He hadn't shared with anyone where he was going. In his pocket was a piece of newspaper folded up and containing a second piece of newspaper, one with holes punched over it. Under his arm was a small file, and inside were pieces of paper with handwritten notes on them. He had made a phone call, hours before, and now as evening began to come to a close, he watched the sunset behind the hills, thinking, *What a perfect sight the loch was at this time.'*

He would quite have enjoyed taking a boat out there, casting a rod, though he didn't know what to do with any caught fish. He would enjoy the company of his beloved Jane, but instead this was work, albeit a type of work he wasn't used to. Macleod heard a car pull up a short distance from him. Checking over a shoulder, he saw the black Land Rover with a woman stepping out of the passenger seat. No one accompanied her, and she wore a black skirt just past her knees with a black jacket and white blouse. Given the nip in the air, he was surprised at the heeled shoes she wore. Macleod turned back and looked out into the loch and waited for the woman to join him. She said very little, instead standing beside him and taking in the view as well.

'I really haven't appreciated having my face put out in the front of all this. Do you realise that?' said Macleod.

'We all have our sacrifices, Inspector, and I'm sure Her Majesty thanks you for them. It's a testing time up here in Scotland. I hear there were some more skirmishes today. They're all pockets of anger and resentment from people to each other, and not that long after Christmas as well. Why is that, Inspector? Why is it every Christmas we say, 'Peace to all mankind,' and yet by New Year we're generally kicking the crap out of each other?' Macleod ignored the vulgarity and instead looked down the loch before turning back to the woman.

'Because we don't listen to the message,' he said.

'Oh, it's still in there, the old face being away from the island hasn't made you lose it.'

'It's changed somewhat, shall we say, but let's not get bogged down about me. I have a message from one of your colleagues,' said Macleod. He put his hand inside his pocket and took out the newspaper cutting. 'I've given you a copy of the newspaper it came from because she's punched holes out.'

'Very good,' said Anna, 'but tell me one thing, she gave this to you, she must really trust you?'

'I'd tell you we worked together, but you know that,' said Macleod. 'What you won't know, is was what we went through. Kirsten's a special person, capable of a lot. She was dubious about going into your profession, but I convinced her.'

'Oh?' said Anna. 'Why? I thought you would have wanted to hang on to her, she was that good.'

'You can't hold on to people, you can't keep them back,' said Macleod. 'She suited the work, she would have been good at it. She can handle herself in a way I haven't seen any other officer do, five feet nothing and yet a power pack. She could take on the big boys without even thinking about it.'

'Well, she has been most useful, Inspector.' Anna Hunt opened the newspaper and was examining the clean copy and that with the punched holes. 'Well, that's the most interesting message,' she said. 'I thank you for that.'

'Before you go,' said Macleod, 'here,' and he handed over the folder under his arm.

'What's this?'

'That is all the information my team could dig out on a certain Arab gentleman's body we found. Kirsten had stuffed her hair into the man's mouth. I don't know how many bodies are out there. When they threw them off that cliff, they could have gone under, we got lucky one was washed along to one side. I've covered it all up as an exercise, it wasn't easy. We've tried to keep everything as fresh as we can, but there's no guarantees.'

'Never are guarantees, Inspector. It's one of the things you take on in life, but you've done well, and I thank you for keeping it hushed up and realising that so quickly. You may have saved her life doing that.'

'It did occur to me that she was probably taking a risk passing a message, but look, if you need assistance, this is Kirsten we're talking about. I've stopped any further report of this or what's going on. There are no records on the files and I'm quite happy to play the dummy out front provided you get to the bottom of it, but if Kirsten needs help, we're available. I'll make my whole staff available for her.'

'That's very welcome news, Inspector, and you've done her a great favour; you've kept this quiet, and yes, it is a message from her. Keep appearing on screen, keep telling people you're investigating the murders from before, try and keep everything on a calm level because at the moment, the country seems quite rocked by it all. If this referendum vote goes the wrong way, who knows what might kick off?'

'Which way is the wrong way?' asked Macleod. 'It looks a close call to me.'

'It is and that's what we're all worried about,' said Anna. 'But thank you again, Inspector,' and she turned to walk away.

'That's not a problem,' said Macleod, 'And if you need any help with the celebration.' Anna Hunt turned around immediately. 'I'll keep my eyes and ears out,' said Macleod, 'I'll let you know if anything else comes up, but if you need help, just say.'

'Inspector, if we need help, I'll go to my own services. If they haven't got enough manpower there, I'll go to the military. If they haven't got enough help there, I'll go to the younger end of the police officers. I'm not quite sure what sort of help you or your team could be to us in this, but I thank you for the offer. The best thing for you to do at the moment is to carry out what

Kirsten asked of you, run cover at the front, make sure the people she's after think you're the one coming for them. That way they won't see her. Oh, by the way, Inspector, I do like this location. You could be good at this spy game. You'd certainly make sure every liaison had a spectacular backdrop.'

The woman turned and walked back to her car with the large folder under an arm. Macleod watched the black car disappear before turning back and looking out into the loch. He stepped forward, made his way down to some stones and began skimming some across the water.

Where are you, Kirsten? he thought. *What can I do for you? Anything?* It was no use. She'd never contact him directly. Probably just chance that his team had picked up an investigation of the dead body. There was an uneasiness in Macleod. He didn't like this sort of thing, handwritten notes, nothing recorded. He always thought stuff like that could backfire, but there was a greater unrest within him. Kirsten Stewart was out there alone, possibly operating in the dark. He'd heard about the explosion on the cruise ship and wondered if she had been on board that. There was the child she was allegedly protecting on the Isle of Lewis. That had resolved, from what he could gather, but he knew so little about what she'd really done.

He looked at his watch and realised he'd have a press conference in three hours, once again sitting down to look like a mug in front of the national press, the great Macleod having achieved nothing. *Oh well,'* he thought, *this one's for you, Kirsten,* and he turned back towards his own car.

Chapter 20

Kirsten opened her eyes and looked at the base of the bunk bed above her, Musgrove would be up there. Kirsten thought it was rather late in the morning despite being up the night before. Maybe Darcy hadn't gotten up. Whatever he was doing, he was letting them have quite a long lie.

Kirsten wondered if her message would get through. It was a risk, but she knew anywhere around Inverness, if a body was found, it was usually Macleod that would get called out to it, at least him or one of his team. She was banking that her former colleagues would recognise what was going on.

She slipped out of the bunk, walked over to her wardrobe where she changed quickly into her usual black attire before walking through to the social room that they'd been occupying for the last couple of weeks. Training had been going well, according to Darcy, but he always wanted more. Kirsten decided to fuel up before the day started. She took some yogurt and some muesli, sat down at the table, and began to eat slowly.

Staring across at the large television, she decided to get up and switch it on before resuming her cereal. The news was on, and she waited until the section for Scotland appeared after the main news. Holding her breath, she waited to hear if there was any news about a body being found, but there was nothing, nothing at all.

Had her plan not worked? Had the bodies just drifted off to sea? Had Macleod realised what was going on? Had the team hushed the whole thing up? Would Anna now know what message had been passed on, or were the shoes just simply sitting there? Maybe somebody would pick them up and dump them. Maybe some unsuspecting child would take out the paper, make an aeroplane of it and throw it over the cliff. There were no guarantees with what she'd done. Kirsten reckoned she had to operate on the basis that nobody had got her message.

As she sat there, she heard the door open. Kirsten glanced over her shoulder and saw Donovan entering the room. She turned back to watch the television, and she heard him approach behind. He didn't speak but instead placed his hands on her shoulders. Instantly, her own hands flew up to his, but he started to rub her shoulders, massage them, as he came down close beside her ear.

'Got a feeling we're going to be working closely,' he said. 'I fancy that. I think you do, too. I can smell the excitement off you.'

Kirsten thought about standing up, turning round and simply smacking the man one across the jaw. She didn't want to give him the pleasure, so she ignored him, looking ahead. His hands continued to grind on her shoulders then moved across to her neck. As much as she felt the man was repugnant, she had to hand it to him, he knew how to work shoulders.

'What makes you think we're going to be working together?'

'These explosives, they need somebody to be able to plant them. That thing with hanging on the edge of the car, that's important. All this jumping on we're doing, thirty miles an hour, that's important as well. I think you're going to be working with me, like I say, nice and close.'

Kirsten could feel the breath on her ear, so close as he talked to her.

'Well, just make sure you don't get too overexcited working with me,' she said. 'Wouldn't want you coming a cropper.'

The man laughed almost wickedly, before walking away and finding some food at the side table. 'Why, Nash?' he said. 'Why does he call you Miss Nash?'

'Because he calls you Donovan, Musgrove. Come on, you must know,' said Kirsten.

'Know what?' asked Donovan.

'Mr Darcy, you must have seen that from the TV.' Donovan shrugged his shoulders. 'All the names, they're all Jane Austen characters. That's why we've got them, nothing more, nothing less.'

'Well, aren't you a scholar. I don't read that sort of stuff,' he said. 'I'd much rather be in front of a good horror.'

Kirsten was amused to find Donovan engaging her in almost civil conversation, but when she looked across at him, she could see his eyes still glaring at her. It wasn't the first bit of unwanted attention she'd ever received, needing to know things. She was going to have to play along with him at times.

'Why do you like horror?' asked Kirsten.

'Guts and gore, isn't it? All the horror films, that's what they are. There's always some woman panicking, always afraid, hunted down.'

'You think you're a good hunter,' said Kirsten. She'd always thought there was something strange about horror, especially the movies, always a woman on her own, always vulnerable.

Maybe that's why men liked to see them like that. She was no vulnerable woman, and if Donovan came over thinking that, he'd soon find a fist in his face.

'Anyway,' said Donovan, 'he wants us all in here in half an hour. Apparently, he's going to tell us his big scheme.'

'And obviously wants to blow something up,' said Kirsten. 'That much is a bit obvious. How much damage could you do with those explosives anyway?'

'Oh, plenty, take a couple of houses out if you wanted.'

'Really? That much? They didn't look that big.'

'What do you know about explosives?' asked Donovan.

'Not a lot, but it doesn't look like much.'

'Depends what type it is. That stuff, it's proper. All we got to do is plant it somewhere it can be set to detonate.'

'So what, we're just planting it?' asked Kirsten.

'I don't know, we have to wait and see, but he wants me to set something up remotely. That's why he's using me.'

Kirsten turned her head back to the television. It had changed to some kids' program. She got up, walked over, and switched it off before getting a cry from Donovan indicating he was watching it. Kirsten shrugged her shoulders, switched the TV back on, and walked to the door of the building. Outside, she could see one of the posted guards. She opened the door and the man stepped across.

'I'm only getting some air,' said Kirsten.

'Mr Darcy's rules. Back inside, please.' Kirsten didn't argue, instead making her way back into the main hall. She picked up a magazine, looking for some reason at a set of furniture she'd never buy, but she quickly put it down when Darcy entered the room.

'Donovan, go and get the rest of them. There's a good lad.'

'Donovan says you're going to tell us all what we're doing.'

'That's correct,' said Darcy, 'but let's wait till they're all here. You probably have a good idea already.'

'What? That you're going to blow something up? I think that was pretty obvious.'

'Of course, but do you not know what else we're going to do? I thought you might. You seem quite astute, Miss Nash, maybe a little bit too astute.'

'What's that meant to mean?'

'Well, I've got the brains for this. I just need people to follow out what I'm going to do. Make sure you don't overthink what you're doing. You see, most of the others like killing in an instant. I've seen that, but not you. You're thoughtful, the way you do things. I need to know you're wholly committed to this enterprise. There'll be a lot of English dead after this.'

Inside Kirsten shuddered, but on the outside, she grinned. 'Good. Just glad to be of service.' Kirsten nodded and sat down and was presently joined by the rest of their small group. Darcy connected a laptop to the side of the TV. It had a picture of the Houses of Parliament on it.

'Now then, ladies and gentlemen, look there. That would be a heck of a target, but unfortunately, that's too well-guarded, too hard to hit. Instead, we're going to go here.' He clicked a button and the image changed to the picture of a train.

'We're going to blow up a train?' said Donovan. 'What's the point in that?'

'We're not blowing up any old train,' said, Darcy. 'We're going to attack the Caledonian Sleeper, blow it up as it rides into King's Cross. King's Cross will be packed with commuters. We'll take them all out and we'll do it on the morning of the referendum result.'

'But how? How are we going to do this?' said Donovan. 'We're just going to walk on? We book passage?'

'No,' said Darcy, tapping a button on his laptop. The picture on the screen changed. 'We're going to have a celebration and we're going to do it by jumping on that train. It won't be that fast, just coming out of Doncaster. Most people would be asleep by then. We'll be able to go through the carriages, arming the train with the bombs. Somebody will have to go to the far end. It's where the drivers are and will be at speed. Once we plant the bombs, we'll all come back together. We will have a device onboard to set them off, but clearly, I'd like to get off myself. If the train is still rolling as it crosses into King's Cross, it'll explode. There's a digital link being set up by Mr Donovan to ensure that case.'

'How are we planning to get off?' said Kirsten.

'Watford, it comes into Watford, makes one stop there, the last stop before King's Cross. We got Doncaster. We work through the night to set the train up while everyone is asleep.'

'Is there anyone onboard that makes this special?' asked Mr Bingley.

'Well, it's funny you should say that,' Darcy retorted. 'There'll be at least one government minister on it, and I believe there's a couple of others may be coming down with them. More than that, it'll be what it symbolises. The great train run from Scotland to England. We'll be showing them we never should be down in England again. We'll make our mark, cause a separation of sorts, whether the vote goes our way or not, but I think we'll get it. I think this time we'll have independence, and this will be our celebration of it, our cry to freedom.'

Kirsten could hear Donovan laugh and saw a wicked smile. She tried to put on a grin herself, but inside she was shaking.

So, this was what it was all about. A plan to destroy the sleeper train. They would kill hundreds, especially if the bombs were as big as Donovan was explaining. King's Cross would be packed at that time of the morning. Kirsten had been down before. She knew the train had stopped not that far away from the main hall where people gathered to wait for their train. Other commuter trains would be coming in as well for the morning rush. A part of her began to panic and she tried to breathe easy.

'You're not impressed, Miss Nash,' said Darcy.

'Oh, yes,' she said. 'You've already talked about somebody going down that train at high speed to plant bombs.'

'That's why you're here,' said Darcy. 'You'll be able to handle it. I've watched you on the edge of that car. If you're up there on your own, you're strong enough to look after yourself if somebody tries to interfere. You need to sit down now. I'm going to take you through it in more detail. Time is moving on. First, let me say this. You don't leave here. I've never allowed you to anyway, but don't go outside. We've been on the move. People may come looking for us. As far as they're going to be concerned from a satellite image, they're just going to see a farmhouse. Old, probably abandoned. From now on, we stay indoors. We've got less than a week to go.'

Kirsten watched in fascinated horror as Darcy showed those plans on the screen in front of her. At first, she thought it was a mad notion, the idea of running somebody down a train to plant bombs, especially on the outside of a train that would be back up to speed of seventy or eighty miles an hour. Darcy also noted, someone would come through the front of the train to kill the driver, then to set the controls for the train to run continuously.

'We'll make sure they can't take it over. Pilot it remotely. Then we get off and then we'll make our way back up here. You'll be heroes.'

It took another hour for the rest of the briefing to conclude. Once it had, Kirsten made an excuse that she needed to go for a shower. In reality, she just wanted to get away. Then she stripped off and got underneath the water. She stood thinking about how she was going to prevent this from happening. She could simply take everybody out in the here and now and then make a run for it, but if she got it wrong, the plan could still go ahead. If she lost her life, nobody would be protected. Darcy clearly wasn't going to let anybody outside. She was going to struggle to send a message. What she told them already had given a lot of detail if they'd picked up the note. Detail about the type of people and the threat that was coming, but at that point, she hadn't known what the target was or how to prevent it.

What weak link was there? What could she exploit? Kirsten dried herself down, got changed and began to walk through the farmhouse building. She made her way back into the main room and looked at her fellow cohorts, all five of them, one at a time. She saw that it was going to be hard, hard to break their spirit now. Instead, she decided to go to the doors and the windows and look outside. There were several guards about, but they were all remaining a lot tighter now to the house. Most of them didn't seem to have weapons on them. Maybe they were hidden, because now they looked like farm hand workers. One of them would have to do. She'd have to get a mobile phone off them of some sort. She noticed that a few of them had them because Darcy liked to contact them on the mobile, but quite how she was going to obtain one, pass away a message and then manage to get the phone back to its owner without them realising was going to be quite something else.

Chapter 21

Kirsten tried to act normal but inside she was stewing like crazy, desperate to work out a method of getting a message to the outside world. She knew the target of the attack and in her mind, she kept seeing the number of commuters that would be blown away when the train arrived at its destination at Kings Cross. She had to break out, get free, or else get a message. Maybe her previous message had worked, maybe Anna Hunt would be looking for a farmhouse, maybe they'd been looking for where she was.

Even if the other message got through, that didn't mean they knew where she was. She didn't even know where she was. The cliff that she threw the bodies over she hadn't recognised. The ruined house they'd gone to, unknown to her. Darcy had been brutal about keeping everything secret, and now he'd revealed his plans, he was locking everyone inside, keeping them all together until it was time to go. There was more training in the days ahead but most of it was done inside covering schematics of trains, where a bomb should be laid, the route into Doncaster, how to get on the train there, where to go once they were on board.

As much as she looked, Kirsten could see no room for escape.

She slept in a dorm with five other people and there were guards outside of it. She ate with everyone, she trained with everyone. The only time she was alone, she was inside a shower. Even then there were wafer-thin cubicles beside her, near shower curtains between her and the next person washing.

It had come to the eve of the referendum vote. On the next afternoon, they'd be heading down south, preparing to board the train that would travel through the night. That was also the day of the referendum. As she watched the news, Kirsten could see how heated the debate was. There were marches out on the streets. She recognised Inverness and saw the scuffle across the main bridge of the city. It seemed like tensions were ramping up, and who knew what would happen after the vote had been cast. Scotland had seen referendums before but not in the light of the killing of politicians and the anger and the hatred that it stirred up, the animosity that then went back and forth between two sides desperate not to lose.

Yet above all of that, here on a different level was Darcy, a madman—of that, Kirsten was convinced. For all that, he was a madman who was making his scheme work. After being utterly depressed by the news she watched, Kirsten went to the dorm that night to sleep, aware that the next day she would have to do something.

It was in the middle of the night when she wandered to the bathroom and she realised something. As she passed one of the outside doors, she saw one of the guards on his phone. Carefully she crept to the window, looking left and right, but she could see no one else out there. The guard was talking for a while and then he opened the door to come inside. Kirsten juked back around the hallway and was able to watch him head for the main hall. There were another two guards in there with him and Kirsten remained at the door listening to their conversation.

There were plenty of banalities about life, some boasts about some woman he'd been with, but then he said he was going to the bathroom, and he may be some time. He said it in a jokey fashion. Kirsten thought it was probably true because they seemed to be doing so very little in terms of guarding anyone. Darcy would be asleep wherever else in the house he went to, and the guard seemed very chilled. She stepped back from the doorway, allowing the guard to walk out and head towards the toilets, before walking behind him up on her tiptoes.

She was the perfect image of stealth and reached in with her hand to the guard's pocket as he continued his walk straight ahead to the toilets. She turned to the right and to the front door. It was locked.

Kirsten knelt down in the hallway and looked at the phone before her. She touched the side button on it and the screen lit up. When she went to do something with it, it instantly asked for a pattern to be input.

All right then, she thought, *what should it be?* She did an inward circle seeing if that was the pattern, but it wasn't. Next, she did an X, but again, there was not the pattern. Then, she went for the old favourite of simply a Z and the screen opened up. Kirsten thanked the guard for being one of those people who just picks the most obvious phone patterns ever known.

Now she was stuck. She had a phone, but it was coming from the wrong phone number if she did get a message. He'd also be able to see any of these, so she'd have to do it innocuously. She looked down into his text messages, and there were very few, most of them coming from billing departments or various companies indicating he'd spent money.

So, he doesn't use the text facility, thought Kirsten, but she thought for a while, *but who would I text?* Then, she got an idea. She looked up the internet on the phone for the number for a particular hire car service in Inverness. She then typed in a message direct to the hire car service. Of course, she couldn't give the game away, not completely, she'd have to put it in some sort of a code. Typing in the name McGrath, she asked for a hire car for Duncan's, saying that she hoped it arrived in time at Duncan's because if she didn't, she would be angry.

It was a very cryptic clue but she wondered if a mind close to hers might get it. Kirsten noted that the message had been sent and closed and cleared the SMS from the phone, closing down, and awaited her man coming back out from the toilet. She moved closer to the other side of the door until he emerged from the bathroom and made his way forward to the main hall again. Before he had reached it, Kirsten moved up beside him, deposited the phone, and then stepped away into the quiet. Two minutes later she was back in her bunk. She reckoned everyone else was asleep, at least as far as she could check, after all, she couldn't walk up to them in person looking at them.

As she lay in the dark, Kirsten prayed her message would get through. Hopefully, the man receiving it would have the wit to understand what he was looking at. There was nothing left to do, and she hoped that the guard didn't look at his phone messages to see what had been sent.

* * *

John was in a good mood. The woman who'd lit up his life

for these past months, Hope McGrath, had stayed over at his flat the previous night and currently was sitting in his kitchen, probably eating some toast. He'd had to leave her in his bed half an hour ago. That was the only disappointment of the past twenty-four hours.

Several months ago, John had had a visit from a six-foot-tall redheaded detective sergeant and immediately he had seen someone he wanted to get to know a lot better. He'd asked a question, she'd agreed, and since then, they'd seen more and more of each other, until now, they were quite the item. John thought it quite exciting that he had a girlfriend who worked solving crimes, though he found her boss Macleod a little bit stifling. He had begun to embrace her profession, and she had begun to trust him more and more, divulging those secrets as they lay in the dark. Bit by bit she opened up about what had scared her in the work that she did, what she enjoyed, and of her hopes and fears, and in return, John had told her all about the exciting world of his car-hire business.

When he thought about it, he laughed. What did she want with him? It couldn't be the work he did anyway. Nobody saw the car-hire business as glamorous, and at eight o'clock in the morning, walking into his building, he didn't either. He was first in, made his way across the small office to switch on the heater, and looked out at the cars and the lot in front of him. The young lad would be in soon and be sent out to clean them again, and he switched on the computer waiting to get the day list.

As he did every morning, he picked up the mobile phone looking to see if anybody had texted in any messages. Most people came in by email; after all, it was the easiest form to deal in. You could send them back what they required, answer any questions. There was a normal booking form on site as well that came up on the computer, but he did have the option for people to text him, so every morning, first thing, John would look at the texts in front of him.

When he pressed the button on the smartphone, he was surprised to see a message there. His last one had been over two months ago. Quickly, he unlocked the phone and pressed the button, which would display the message in full, 'Required hire car for McGrath.' He thought *that's funny, it's Hope's name.*

As he continued to read, he became more bemused. 'Taxi to go to Duncan's.' *Duncan who?* he thought. 'Hope it will arrive in time.' *Well, not if I don't know where I'm going.* 'And I'm going to be angry if I don't get there.'

In his head, John was saying this was a prank call, but the name McGrath on it made him think. John wondered if someone had got wind of him being Hope's boyfriend and was now sending provocative messages to her through his phone. Either way, he'd better check it out, and so John went to his desk, picked up his normal phone, and rang Hope's mobile.

'Hey, gorgeous. Can you not leave me alone for a half-hour beauty sleep?' he heard her say.

'I'm not that desperate,' he said, 'but I've got something you need to know.'

'What?'

'Well, I've just come in checking my text messages because occasionally, we get one that comes in looking to book a car or that, and somebody's written to you.'

'Me?' said Hope, 'In what way precisely?'

'They've labelled it McGrath, and then they've also said they want to go to Duncan's. Then, there's the best of it. If they don't get there on time, they'll be angry.'

John could hear Hope giving out a little bit of a chuckle, but then she suddenly went serious, 'Say that to me again.'

'Told you. Name McGrath, says they're going to Duncan's, don't want to be late. If they do, be angry.'

'Forward that text to me,' said Hope, 'Right now. I need to get the exact words.'

'What's the matter?' asked John. 'I thought this was some sort of hoax. I was just ringing you so you could get these people to stop annoying my phone.'

'Take the number down it was sent from as well, text me that too,' said Hope.

'Okay,' said John, 'I will do, and by the way, while you're here, do you want to meet for lunch?'

'I won't be available for lunch,' said Hope. 'I'm going to be with Macleod.'

'Has he found you already?'

'No, John. What you've just given me, I need to take it to the inspector.'

* * *

Seoras Macleod had dressed quickly, brushed his hair, put his tie on, and made it into the office in the space of half an hour. When he got in, Hope was already sitting there inside the internal office while his other colleagues waited outside in the main office. 'Run that past me again,' said Macleod, 'from the top.'

'John got a text message onto his work phone.'

'His work phone,' said Macleod. 'Where's the number of that work phone?' He made his way to the front door of his office, opened it, and shouted out to Ross who was waiting outside.

'Ross, take down this number,' Macleod said it to him, 'I want to know where you can find this number out on the internet. Where you can find it anywhere.'

But then he closed the door with a thump, made his way back to the desk, sat down and stared at the piece of paper in front of him. Hope McGrath pointed to the paper.

'Hire car for McGrath and then that the person hopes it arrives in time at Duncan's. And if not, they'll be angry. It all sounds a bit funny, but because it's got my name on it, that's just a bit strange. I thought I should follow it up.'

Macleod didn't say anything, staring simply at the words in front of him.

'Sir, Seoras. What's up? Are you okay? You seem a bit distracted.'

'Shush,' said Macleod, 'just shush.' He picked up the paper and began to pace around his office. Two minutes later, Ross poked his head in, 'You can get it almost anywhere on the internet. If you look up John's taxi company, that's where it is. Anybody could have got that.'

'Thank you,' said Macleod, and began to pace about again.

'Are you okay? Do you want me to get you a drink or something?' said Hope, and then Macleod clicked his fingers picking up, 'I need to talk to Anna Hunt,' he said.

* * *

It was eleven o'clock when Anna Hunt arrived at the side of Loch Ness. The day was overcast and the light was no longer dancing across the water, but rather it was flat on the dreariest of days, but she made her way towards the shore. Macleod didn't look around and he didn't even engage in conversation as Anna stood beside him. Instead, he handed over a piece of paper. After a moment, Anna Hunt turned to him, 'And what's this?'

'Transcription. What we found on the phone of a certain car-hire salesman. It becomes of note because McGrath is my sergeant. She did not send that message. She's unaware of anyone who would and she doesn't know what it means.'

Anna Hunt looked at it. 'And in truth, I don't know what it means, either,' she said.

'Indeed, you may not but I'll tell you this: it's telling me something,' said Macleod.

'I saw, Inspector.'

'It's deliberately sent to McGrath. It's somebody who knows McGrath,' said Macleod, 'But it also says she hopes to arrive in time at Duncan's. If they don't, they'd be angry. Duncan, one of the kings of Scotland and she'll be angry, cross. This is Kirsten,' said Macleod, 'I know her. It's the way she thinks.'

'You not just reading that into it?' said Anna Hunt, intrigued but sceptical.

'No, this is from her all right.'

'So, they're going to make an attack,' said Anna.

'It looks like it. I guess you would need to get moving.'

'I think I do,' said Anna, 'Thank you for your assistance. So, King's Cross,' said Anna, 'but the message doesn't say when.'

'The referendum is just about here,' said Macleod, 'I think it's any time from now.'

'I better run then,' said Anna Hunt, 'Good work, Inspector. Your stature is growing minute by minute.'

Macleod turned around to chastise the woman for being so cheeky but when he did, he stopped and watched her stride purposefully into the car. She turned and looked at him as the car sped away and he thought he saw the briefest hint of a smile. Mind you, it was the briefest.

Chapter 22

Kirsten could sense no change in Darcy's mood towards her and thought she'd got away with using the text on the guard's phone. It wasn't long before she had to effectively pack up, although they weren't taking anything with them. Darcy said to leave their original clothes behind and instead lay down their black garb that they'd trained in for the last couple of weeks. There was a solemnness amongst them all as they realised the job was coming. But when she looked across Donovan, he was grinning.

'After the celebration, we'll come back and do some proper celebrating,' said Donovan, looking at Kirsten. 'Darcy said he's going to treat us real good.'

'I don't think that's likely, more like a few beers holed up somewhere,' said Kirsten. 'After all, if we're going to set bombs off, people are going to come looking for us.'

'It's all right, I don't need somewhere full of splendour. You'll be there, won't you?' said Donovan, giving her a wink. The man was repugnant, but more than that, he actually believed that he was touching some sort of part of Kirsten that might respond.

'Whatever,' she said and turned to look at Mr Bingley,

entering the room with Mr Wickham.

'Darcy says to get your backsides into gear. We should get out in five minutes; he's going to torch this place.'

I bet he is, thought Kirsten, *but he'd have to do it quietly. He can't just have a massive fire going and get out of here. He'd have to leave his people behind.*

Kirsten made her way towards the front door of the farmhouse, finding it to be open for the first time in weeks. She walked unaccompanied right into the small space in front of the farmhouse where a black van was waiting.

'Ah, Miss Nash,' said Darcy. 'That's your transport, in there with the rest of us. It's a long ride down to Doncaster. The sooner you get in, the sooner you get comfortable. Find your own spot. No need for a blindfold this time; you know where we're going.'

Kirsten gave a simple nod. Darcy looked at her quizzically. 'You're not excited?'

'I'm just being thorough,' said Kirsten. 'Don't want to get overexcited about this. Get excited when the job's done.'

'That's a good attitude,' said Darcy. 'Do you not feel it flowing through your veins though? Blow for Scotland, that's what this is. You understand, don't you? Kicking the teeth of the English oppressors.'

English oppressors, thought Kirsten. She wasn't quite sure he could use that anymore. Instead, she gave a simple nod. In her time in Scotland, Kirsten had met many nationalists, most of them wanting to fight for a government that was wholly their own. As much as she might not have been minded to or pushed for it in any particular way, she never resented them, never thought them dangerous. They were just following an agenda to give them a parliament they wanted.

But Darcy was different. Darcy, like all crazy people, wanted to make something happen, force it to happen, whether people had wishes or not. The point of a parliament surely was to be there for the good of the people. Darcy seemed to be ignoring the people or certainly calling the people a very select few, something that had always been done through history.

Kirsten clambered inside the van, wrapping a black hair tie on the back of her head to produce a ponytail, and she took a seat at the back of the van. She saw the rest of the team get in, Harris at the front with Bingley, Musgrove sitting beside Wickham, and Donovan came to sit close to Kirsten.

'I got your back,' he said as he sat down.

'Just do your job,' said Kirsten. 'I don't care what you've got.' She couldn't quite understand this attitude from him. Whatever happened, she was going to keep an eye on him. Darcy approached and stuck his head into the back of the van.

'Now don't worry about this place. The boys I'm leaving will take care of it. I'm sorry about your belongings because you've all worked incredibly hard. That's a small sacrifice. We'll make sure you're geared up where we're going afterwards.'

'And where is that exactly?' asked Donovan.

'I'll tell you that once we're getting off the train. If I say it now and you get caught, they'd come for us. I ran this place with discretion. I ran it so nobody knows who I am, where I am. . .'

'Nobody will know who you are and where you are either. Let's settle down because it's a long dark ride for us. Before we start, here.' He turned away and then turned around, throwing a box into the van. 'Sandwiches and drinks. Grab them now because you won't see them once we start.'

Kirsten reached forward, started pulling out sandwiches

and throwing them around the van. Then she passed drinks around. Darcy nodded in approval before shutting the door, leaving them in blackness.

'I think I've got mustard on my hand,' said Donovan.

'Lick it off,' said Harris, 'and shut up. Just try and get some rest on the way down.'

Kirsten struggled to rest. In her mind, she tried to go over how she was going to play her part in this charade. They were to jump onto the train as it pulled out of Doncaster. From there, she was to clamber up top, move her way along, get to the far end and plant the bombs that she carried on her. She still couldn't believe how small an amount of explosive was compared to the damage. Darcy said it would do. Maybe she could get to the far end, warn the driver before he was taken out. Get him to get a message to his bosses. Maybe her other message had got through. She only hoped that McGrath's boyfriend had the wit to know where to send the message to, only hoped that McGrath herself could take it to Macleod. He was on Kirsten's wavelength. He'd understand it straight away, or at least after a little bit of thought.

When the door opened again, it was dark outside. Kirsten, along with the five other terrorists, climbed out of the van, realising they were close to the tracks. Darcy stepped out of the van, and it sped off leaving just them there. Donovan carried a backpack, but otherwise, everyone had a belt which carried a certain number of explosives. Kirsten wasn't armed but that didn't mean all the rest weren't. That time they'd gone for the Arabs, Harris had been given a gun.

'Okay, it's leaving in approximately five minutes. As it comes along, we do as we trained, jumping on towards the back. From there, some of us will move through the carriage from the back.

Miss Nash will get forward once we have the bombs planted, and we route back to meet again. Then we discuss further how this works. Remember, as long as the train gets to King's Cross, it will explode. Mr Donovan has rigged up a GPS detonator. If that detonator arrives, the explosives will go off.'

The group nodded at Darcy, and he led them along a path and under a fence to an open piece of track, and crouched down in the darkness until Darcy gave the word. As they waited, the front end of the sleeper train came through and Kirsten watched as Harris, who was at the rear of the group, was the first to jump on the end of the train. The others followed. The rear door, wide enough for a single person, magically opened. There was a moment of scare when Donovan seemed to slip, but Darcy grabbed him and pulled him inside. Kirsten was the last one through and she suddenly came face to face with a woman working for the sleeper company.

'This is Jennifer,' said Darcy. 'Jennifer's a true patriot. She's done extremely well using a device that enabled her to keep this rear door open without alerting the rest of the train. I think we all want to turn and thank Jennifer for her service.'

Kirsten saw a girl with black ringlets tied around the back, dressed in a smart waistcoat and trousers. She beamed at Darcy, and he turned to her announcing 'Scotland forever.'

'Scotland forever,' the girl said in an excited whisper.

Darcy reached out and grabbed her by the throat. 'And Scotland thanks you for your sacrifice.' With a strong left arm, he threw her off the train out through the open single door.

'You probably killed her,' said Kirsten.

'Indeed,' he said, 'but her sacrifice will not be in vain, unlike yours, Miss Nash, or who are you, exactly?' Kirsten went to react, but Darcy pulled a gun on her, pointing it straight at her chest.

'Oh, no, you don't. It was only this morning we found it. A text message sent for a hire car. Why were you contacting a car hire company, Miss Nash, in the name of McGrath?'

'It's my name,' said Kirsten. 'When we're done, I need the car to get back to Ireland.'

'Who's Duncan then?'

'Duncan's, it's the pub. They're local. They know it. They've been shabby before. That's why I said I would be angry.'

Darcy stepped forward with the gun, and turned Kirsten around. She thought at first, she was going to be thrown off the train. 'No,' said Darcy when he saw her glancing the way to the open door. 'Problem is if I get that wrong, you survive, you warn everybody what's going on. No. Instead,' he grabbed the back of her neck and shoved her against the interior wall of the train, 'for you, you're getting a free ticket to the big celebration.'

He took a pair of handcuffs out of his back and slapped one onto one of Kirsten's wrists. He slapped the other one behind her on the other wrist, pressed the door, and opened one of the cabins at the rear of the train. He threw Kirsten in and told Harris to go in and watch her. 'Trip's over, Nash. Pity, you could certainly be an operator. Maybe you are an operator, but for who? Not that it matters. They can pick up your body pieces once we get to King's Cross.'

'How are you going to get all your bombs planted on this train?'

Darcy reached forward and grabbed the explosives off Kirsten before throwing them on the ground. He stamped on them.

'As if I suspected someone and was going to hand them live explosives. Harris, stay. The rest of you, outside now for a new plan.' Kirsten could hear instructions being given as to how the train must be taken over and soon she heard people on the move. Harris made her lie down in one of the bed bunks, face down, arms behind her in a most uncomfortable position. Further than that, he stood at a distance, gun pointed at her.

'You're not even Scottish, are you? You're Irish,' he said. 'Is that why you betrayed us? I never trusted them. They say they're fighting for a cause, free of the English, but it's not the same. You did a deal, didn't you, back then? You did a deal.'

'This isn't freedom, is it? Blowing people up? It's ridiculous. Harris, he'll kill you after this as well. I tell you that now. Look at him, they've killed everybody. He doesn't care about you. If you had lost in that rectangle we were trying to fight in, you'd be gone. He killed everyone in there. You know that, don't you?'

'It was their sacrifice. He needed people.'

'He knew they would die!'

'They were people who were strong, and you betrayed them,' said Harris. 'I betrayed no one.'

'He's betraying his own country.'

Harris stepped forward, struck Kirsten at the rear of her head with the back of the gun. She nearly swore into the bed close beneath her, feeling the blood trickling past her mouth.

'That'll be enough talk,' said Harris. 'Just lie there and contemplate your last few hours. It'd probably go by quite quickly.'

Kirsten struggled to think what to do. In her current position, she couldn't even react quick enough to get to Harris before he shot her. With her hands incapacitated, it made it all the more difficult. One thing she knew was how to kick, but she'd have to wait for the right moment because she'd have to follow it up, and besides, she wasn't sure if Harris had the key to even get her out of her handcuffs.

It was some two hours later before Darcy made a reappearance, handing a bottle of water over to Harris. Then he turned to Kirsten.

'Everyone's in position. It's been done,' said Darcy. 'You've caused me to change my plans. We were all going to get off at Watford, let it run into the station and blow up, but now we'll be doing a jump at the last second, make sure it gets there just in case you've warned anyone. You didn't get through with the message, did you?'

'What message? I'm from Ireland, I'm not a spy. I'm all for independence, but I'm not a lunatic. Won't do any good killing all these people. It only breeds resentment. Look at us. We couldn't get the best of them in thirty years.'

'You gave up,' said Darcy. 'Most disappointing. One thing I don't like, Miss Nash, is being betrayed.'

Darcy came in close, putting his hands around Kirsten's throat. He started to squeeze, trying to choke her. Kirsten was aware that he wasn't very good at it. She pretended to struggle for breath as he said into her ear, 'The train rolls on, you with it. I wish I could stay and watch you get your comeuppance. I wish we could take you with us, give you proper hiding to teach you, but whatever you're here for and whatever you are, it's too late. We have control of the train. I've got lots of people peacefully sleeping as they head off to their doom. Once we get past Watford, I'll take out the guard. Feel free to have a sleep though,' said Darcy. 'Don't worry, we'll wake you up. I might even bring you down the front. You can have a front-row seat, see King's Cross as it goes up in flames. I'm good like that,' he said. 'I look after my people.'

He slapped her on the side of the face and Kirsten stared back at him.

'Keep an eye on her, Mr Harris. Make sure she doesn't go anywhere.'

Kirsten watched Darcy leave the room and then glanced back at Harris who just kept staring at her. She had time, she had hours, but she was so securely looked after, she didn't know how she'd break free.

Chapter 23

'W'e've done a quiet search everywhere, ma'am. We can't find anything. There's just nothing here.' Anna Hunt looked at the police sergeant advising her on how the search for any explosives was going on.

'There's nothing unusual about King's Cross Station. They've been at it through the night and in the previous evening. Maybe we scared them off, ma'am. We've tried to be discreet, but it's not that easy to keep yourself hidden away when you're trying to search everywhere.'

'That's understood, sergeant,' said Anna Hunt, 'but it's got me no further forward. This is the place. It will happen today, trust me. Keep searching.'

'We could always evacuate the place.'

'But we don't know when it's coming.'

Anna Hunt stepped away from the sergeant and made her way up to a transit van and climbed into the rear of it. On the outside, it looked like a bakery delivery company, but inside Justin Chivers was sitting at a large row of computers, looking through many screens.

'I've tapped into the surveillance system at King's Cross, but I'm not spotting anything either. We've got police eyes on it.

Everyone's been alerted. There's just nothing there.'

'I wonder if they're bringing anybody in. There are so many trains coming in. How are we doing with covering them off?'

'Well, we have various operatives joining the early morning trains. Nobody's noticed anything suspicious.'

'What about the train from Scotland, the overnight sleeper? I take it you covered that off, Justin.'

'Yes, ma'am. We had direct communication with the driver, and all was well.'

'Okay. Keep checking. We need to work out where this is going. By the way, have they announced the result yet?'

'Not yet, but I think it's close. They're recounting it.'

'That's all we need. Anyway, we don't win or lose whatever the result of that is. We win or lose depending on what happens at King's Cross.'

Justin Chivers nodded and began searching through the screens again. Behind him in the corner, glancing at her own screens, was Carrie Anne. Her arm was still in a sling, but Justin reckoned her eyes would make up for any lack of mobility that she had.

'Any thoughts in the corner?' asked Anna Hunt.

'We've got the bases covered. I'm not sure what else we can do. The sleeper's coming down and we checked it at every station. The driver's given us a thumbs up. There's nothing untoward as far as I can see.'

'I guess it's up to Kirsten then, wherever she is. Come on, Stewart, give us a sign.'

* * *

Kirsten could not move her wrists out of the handcuffs. She

could feel them cutting into her whenever she tried, and there was always the ever-watchful Harris looking at her. She felt the train come to a halt and realised by the daylight outside they must have been going through Watford.

The door of the cabin opened, and Darcy put his head in. Kirsten noted that he had on the uniform of the serving staff on the train.

'Okay, Harris, that's us past Watford. When the train gets moving again, you might want to take her out, handcuff her in the corridor, then she can see the disaster happening. I'd hate this to be the last thing she sees. Much better if she saw the whole thing being blown apart.'

'Of course, sir,' said Harris. 'And when are we getting out?'

'I'll be back for you. Don't worry. It's quite close in. We have to make sure the train gets there.'

'Of course,' said Harris. 'I wasn't suggesting anything else.'

'Good,' said Darcy. The train began to move again. As the door shut for the last time, he said, 'Got passengers waking up. We've let the couple off at Watford that needed to, but we're still a full load. They won't suspect anything.'

'They'll be here,' said Kirsten.

'What do you mean, they'll be here?'

'They'll be here. You wait and see.'

'Here,' said Darcy to Harris. 'That's the key to her cuffs. Just make sure you got the gun on her when you take her outside, then cuff her up.'

'Of course, boss.'

Kirsten watched Darcy leave the room. The door of the room didn't close fully, but Darcy continued on his way. Harris stood watching it as the door flapped several times.

'Are you going to sort that out? That'll rattle all the way in,' said Kirsten.

'Does it annoy you?' said Harris. 'If so, good.'

Kirsten looked around. She was underneath another bunk and would barely have enough room to sit up if she was facing the right way. The passage between the bunk and the sidewall of the cabin was tight, but Harris was smart enough to keep himself at the far end where the sink was.

Kirsten remembered being on the sleeper before, but nowadays it was much smarter, although back then, you had a cup of tea brought to you and a sort of croissant. The door rattled again, swinging open as the train went round the bend.

'Oh, that's going to do your head in,' said Kirsten, 'really going to do your head in.'

'Shut up,' said Harris.

'It's not a good idea anyway, somebody could walk by.'

'Who's going to walk by?' said Harris. 'We control the train now.'

'No, you don't control it. All you've done is take away the people who are working in it. Darcy said they let people off at the last station. That was clever. He's probably got somebody up with the driver. That's why it's continuing. Threatened the man, probably told him that his wife and kids are being held at gunpoint, or maybe he hasn't told him the full story about the explosives. That's what they do. What are you, Harris? Ex-army?'

'We don't talk about our earlier life.'

'No, you don't. That was another one of his because if you did, you might get to talking. If you're army, you were protecting people. This isn't. This is murder.'

'Shut up,' said Harris. 'I don't want to hear it. This is the English we're talking about.'

'Half the people in this train are going to be Scottish, if not more,' said Kirsten. 'Are you going to make a point by blowing up our own people? Where did you get that?' She had dropped her Irish accent now and let her Highland note come in. 'Your accent,' said Harris.

'Yes. Inverness born and bred,' said Stewart. 'I work for the services, and they'll be coming. He might say he's getting you to jump off, but he won't be. Besides, you know how he works. He'll shoot you, then he'll get off himself.'

'You're just trying to do my head. That's all you're trying to do,' The door slammed several times, 'and that thing's doing my head,' he said.

Harris made his way across the edge of the bunk towards the door to close it. Kirsten rolled over and let go an almighty kick to his chin. The man tumbled, falling to the floor. She rolled herself off the cabin bed to jump behind him, dropping her knees onto his back. When he continued to struggle, she stood up and kicked him several times in the back of the head.

She could see he was out cold, not moving, and she dropped herself down and began to search his pockets. The movement was awkward because her hands were behind her, locked in the cuffs, but she knew she'd have to be quick in case anyone came into the room.

As she was down on his prone position, she reached inside his back pocket and felt something cold and metallic. As her hands ran over it, she recognised the key. *That's the one*, she thought, and nimbly worked her hands around to undo her cuffs.

Kirsten carefully put her head out of the door and looked down the train corridor. There was no one there. She closed the door behind her and started moving down, when suddenly the door in front of her opened. She tensed up, hands at the ready, but an elderly face popped out. 'Do we get up now? Do we have to go and sort ourselves?'

'Stay in the cabin. Don't come out,' said Kirsten.

'Why, dear? Who are you? You're all dressed in black.'

'Exactly,' said Kirsten. 'Now get back in the cabin.'

She forcibly pushed the woman in and closed the door behind her. Kirsten moved quickly along the corridor into the next carriage ahead of her. As she was transferring from one to the other, she saw a head pass by the window in front of her. Carefully, she closed the door from behind and looked around the corner. Kirsten could see someone in a steward's uniform. From the back, the hair looked like Bingley.

The man was stocky and wouldn't be easy to take out, so Kirsten walked down behind him carefully. As soon as she was near and sure she wasn't making a noise, she threw her arm around him, choking him, slowly taking him to the floor. As she held him, there was a cry from the far end of the train and Kirsten could see Musgrove, with a gun in her hand.

She fired and Kirsten dropped. The bullet caught Bingley somewhere around the chest area, pushing him backwards, and he fell over Kirsten, who was tight to the ground. The train at this point was travelling along at a reasonably gentle pace because it would be coming into London soon. Maybe there was another four or five miles to go.

Kirsten began to crawl on the floor quickly as she heard shots being fired over the top of her head. She ducked around the corner again, knowing that Musgrove would be coming up the train corridor. As she disappeared out of sight, Kirsten felt the train begin to move. It was picking up speed in a violent way. Musgrove must've had a connection through to Darcy or whoever was in the front carriage.

Kirsten opened a window. Then she knelt down, waiting for Musgrove to come around the corner. When she did, the gun was high, expecting Kirsten to be standing up. From below, Kirsten drove up straight into the ribs of Musgrove, pushing her back and pushing her off the carriage wall. The gun fell from her hand and the woman tumbled to the ground, Kirsten on top of her.

There came another cry and further down the corridor now was Wickham. He too pulled a gun out and Kirsten grabbed the prone Miss Musgrove, pulling her over herself. There were a couple of shots and Kirsten heard them thud into the body of the woman in front of her.

Kirsten tried to drag her back down the corridor with her, using her as a human shield. She could hear the woman croaking. Clearly, she'd been shot but Kirsten didn't care, moving herself back around the corner. She knew there was a gun, one that had fallen when Musgrove had been hit by Kirsten's shoulder.

It took Kirsten two seconds to work out what she was going to do. Wickham would be less than halfway down the corridor, so Kirsten turned the corner, rolled forward towards the gun, and picked it up. As she came up to her feet, she fired four times in rapid succession and watched as Wickham was hit by each bullet, twice in the head, and the man dropped.

She could hear rumblings in the cabins, but she shouted at everyone to stay inside as she now sprinted down the corridor. They were well inside London, and she could see the tall buildings on either side. Soon they'd be at the station.

Kirsten charged for all she was worth, moving into the next carriage. The train was long and she'd have at least ten or twelve to go through. The next five minutes were the longest of her life as she kept running down corridors, suddenly having to pull out a gun when she saw someone moving from a cabin. Every time, it was just someone on their holiday or down for a business meeting, but always someone who was now petrified.

She yelled at them to get back in, shoved them when they didn't, and kept up her pace. Eventually, Kirsten reached one of the forward carriages that held the single seats for those who slept in a seat through the night. Ahead of it would be the guard compartment. She glanced at the window and noticed the explosives that were outside. The explosives were not secreted here and maybe they'd just been put out now that they were coming closer.

'Who put those there?' she shouted. The people on the seats looked petrified, and then someone pointed towards the guard carriage. The door slid open. Donovan stepped out, firing shots at her. Kirsten was in a carriage full of people and she had to get to him quick.

'No, you don't,' he shouted, and held up what looked like a detonation button. 'I'll blow it now. I really will.'

Some people would have taken a moment to think. They would have realised the panic inside, all the lives at stake, and before them was a madman about to press a button. Some would've wondered about whether or not Donovan would have been ready to kill himself. None of these thoughts came through Kirsten's head. Instead, the hand reacted. The gun went up, and two shots later, Donovan was lying on the floor.

She stepped over and realising she'd only caught him in the shoulder and neck. Bending down, she screamed at him for the detonator and ripped it from his hand.

'That's not the only detonator,' said Donovan. 'You're too

late. We're hurtling in. As soon as we reach the station, we blow up anyway.'

Kirsten could hear the panic in the people behind her. As she turned, she handed a man the weapon and told him to point it to Donovan. She doubted Donovan would move anyway. He was too badly injured, but always best to have somebody there in case he tried something.

Kirsten ran through the guard compartment before opening up the entrance to the train driver's cabin. Through a window, she could see in the corner the original driver of the train lying against the wall, his neck in a weird angle. In the driver's seat, she recognised the back of Darcy's head. Kirsten reached forward, arms going around Darcy's neck, and she found he didn't resist.

'You're too late,' he said, 'much too late. Into the first platform, that's where he put it,' gasped Darcy. 'That's when we all go boom. It's close enough you see. We're sealed now, sealed in. I've shut all the doors. I've pulled everything. You can't open the outside doors.'

'Where is it? Where's the detonation box?'

'As if I'm going to tell you.'

'It's with you here, isn't it? It's up here in the front of the train. You're looking to die, so you brought it and kept it with you just to make sure.'

'You're smart at times, aren't you?' said Darcy. Kirsten held the man's neck tight, looking around. She saw a box on the ground. 'That box,' she shouted.

Darcy laughed. 'You'll never be able to force it out the gaps between the carriages. Like I say, we're practically sealed in.'

Kirsten looked out the window in front of her. There were high buildings in either side, but she was sure down the tracks she could see the station coming. She squeezed Darcy's neck tighter then realised that the man was hanging on, forcing her to work on him instead of stopping the train. She snapped his neck and let him fall from the seat before she sat down and pulled back on every brake the train had.

The train screamed but still hurtled forward. When she saw the station ahead, she believed there was no way it could stop in time. Kirsten reached over and grabbed the box that contained the GPS detonator. It was cumbersome and awkward, but she put it in her arms and begun to run. She had to get it off the train, but there was only one door that still opened. One door had been overridden, and it was at the back of the train.

Kirsten took off for all she was worth, screaming at people to get clear. She kept running, racing past door after door, cabin after cabin. She hurdled Wickham lying on the ground and then she looked out of the window. She began to see the 'Welcome to King's Cross' signs. They hadn't reached the first platform, but they wouldn't be far from it.

As she reached the last carriage, Kirsten ran hard. She was able to get to the end but saw that the door was still hard shut. She put the box down and pulled on the door. It gradually opened, a tight squeeze, but soon she thought she had enough to get the box clear. She turned to reach for it, but something struck her in the face. She looked up to see Harris.

'You won't stop us. This is all going up,' he said. She stepped forward, punching several times, but the man was good, casting a kick to her side before catching her with a hard fist to the head. Kirsten shook it off, turned and grabbed the box, making her way towards the door.

'No, you won't,' he cried. 'No, you won't,' and Kirsten tried to throw the box. It landed on the edge of the door, part of it hanging out. She could see another 'Welcome to King's Cross' sign.

'That's us,' laughed Harris. 'That's us here. You tried hard, but we're going to deliver a right thrashing to these English.'

Kirsten dove forward but felt a hand grab her foot. She ended up just shy of the box. Turning, she saw Harris's face, his hand on her foot. She took the other foot, kicked hard four times straight into his head. The hand eventually relaxed, and Kirsten turned, pushing hard off Harris's head, her fingers outstretched, and she pushed the box. Slowly, it tipped, the train coming towards a halt, and then it dropped off the back. A few seconds later, the train stopped.

Kirsten was able to get up, jump on the back of Harris and hold him tight. As she did so, a police officer leapt onboard, pulled a gun at her, and Kirsten held her hands up. He pushed her to the ground and another officer took care of Harris.

'Let her up,' said a voice that Kirsten recognised. She looked up and saw Anna Hunt standing in her skirt and black jacket. 'What's the situation, Stewart?' she asked.

'We've got bombs onboard. I've disabled the terrorists but it was a GPS signal.'

'Where is it?'

'I knocked it out the back of the train.' She stood up with Anna Hunt and they jumped off the train, running along the last bit of platform. They got to the edge and Kirsten looked down to see the box of the GPS controller sitting two metres beyond the end of the platform. Kirsten started to hyperventilate and Anna Hunt looked at her.

'What? What's the matter?'

'Don't move that box. If it comes two metres closer, then everything goes boom.'

Chapter 24

The black van advertising a bakery outside King's Cross station remained there for most of the day. Inside, a woman dressed all in black sat on her backside in the far corner.

'So, you got it,' said Justin, 'you managed to get through.'

'Two metres Justin, two metres, and I was gone, all of them were gone, you might have been gone too. I don't know how big that explosion would have been.'

'But you got it!'

A woman came down and started to brush Kirsten's hair. She looked up and saw the smiling face of Carrie Anne. 'You came through—well done.'

The rear door opened, and Anna Hunt stepped up into the back of the van. 'Well, I'll be damned,' she said.

'What?' asked Justin.

'Kirsten dispatched our ringleader at the front of the train. He goes by the name of Arnold, Arnold Pasco, but his real name is Donald Macritchie. He left home at the age of sixteen, born and bred in Scotland, but he fell out with his father. Looks like he killed him in the end.'

'Come again?' asked Justin.

'Angus Macritchie was killed on the orders of his son. He always thought he'd simply disappeared and run off to London, but we've been tracing his activities for a while, but we never thought he would've been involved in this.'

'He covered his tracks well,' said Kirsten. 'He killed people after he used them for what he needed, killed them. Probably the soundest way of making sure he never got caught. There'll be a farmhouse up in some hills somewhere that have been put to the torch. I imagine everyone who used to guard it is now dead. He brought nearly thirty people in to reduce it to a team of six, I'm convinced he shot the rest. We'll have a bit of clean-up work to do.'

'Clean-up work's fine,' said Anna Hunt, 'The key thing at the moment is we stopped this train from going boom. London's impressed with you again.'

'I couldn't give a stuff about London.'

'It's dominating the news though,' said Justin, 'I can bring it up if you want?'

'I just want to go to sleep,' said Kirsten. 'Did we get everyone off the train? I mean, did we pick up any of the terrorists who were left?'

'We got a hold of the guy you called Harris, he's been put away. He's not speaking yet, but he will. Don't worry; we'll get into this,' said Anna, 'clean it up. I'm not going to put that on your squad now. You're all a little bit battered.'

'How's Dom by the way?' asked Kirsten.

'Oh, he'll live,' said Carrie Anne. 'It's going to be another month or two before he's back with us, but he's fine.'

'I see you've still got that sling on your arm,' said Kirsten.

'That'll be another month,' said Carrie Anne, 'Well, I'll still come in, make the coffee for you.'

'What I don't get,' said Kirsten, 'is how nuts this guy was. He was quite happy that even if they got the referendum result, they just go down and blow people up. He could drive people back with that, turn around and say, "Let's come together." Wasn't a lot of logic in what he was doing.'

'He was a fervent nationalist, extremist. He wasn't like those people you see on the TV,' said Anna, 'There's plenty of them about forcing their will on people. You've got to give them an election, give them a fighting chance.'

'It's not like you can rig an election,' said Justin, and then he began to laugh in a way that Kirsten wondered just what had ever gone on before.

'Enough of that,' said Anna. 'We don't talk like that. Anyway, I've got to go and see London, see the prime minister, and tidy things up. I expect you three to get your backsides back up to Inverness. I've got a station up there with nobody in it, and, Justin, you owe me a lot of people who are currently working for you up there, make sure you get them south.'

'They'll be on the next train,' said Justin. Anna Hunt walked over to Kirsten and extended a hand. Kirsten reached up and shook it.

'Well done, Stewart. Guess you can have tomorrow off.'

'Is that a promise?'

'Okay. Yes,' said Anna, 'I promise.'

'I want to jet up, get me a jet from Northolt somewhere up to Inverness so I can actually have tomorrow off instead of travelling.'

'You got a date or something, someone to meet?' Kirsten stopped, staring at Anna, and looked off behind her to the screens.

'Do you know what? I do,' she said. 'I do, somebody give me

a mobile.'

* * *

Kirsten sat nursing her jaw before drinking a slug of the coffee that was sitting in the cup in front of her. She was sitting out on the Inverness street, sitting on one of two seats round a small table. She was dressed in her trainers, jogging bottoms, with a hoodie over a crop top underneath. She'd been out for a brief run, but now she was stopped waiting for her guest to arrive. She picked up her mobile phone while she was waiting. She thought it best to contact someone but she was unsure of his response.

'Seoras,' said Kirsten, when a man answered the phone at the other end.

'Kirsten, so you're alive then? I guess that was you down in London.'

'Can't talk about that,' said Kirsten. 'I thought you understood that by now but look, Seoras, thank you for all your help.'

'I looked like a bit of a mug,' he said, 'being on TV, couldn't find this, couldn't find that, and now we have people performing heroics on trains in London. You don't mind going on the telly and tell them that I was stalling for you, that I was just keeping everything going?'

'Can't do that, Seoras,' said Kirsten, smiling. 'I'm sat in Inverness now,' she said. 'Sat on my day off, having a coffee.'

'Where?' he asked. 'Name it and I'll be there.'

'I'm sorry,' she said, 'I've got someone special coming.'

'You mean Anna Hunt? Fair play to her. She acted on everything I said to her.'

'It's not Anna,' said Kirsten. 'At the moment, I need a little bit of me-time, someone that's going to boost my soul. That's a phrase you'd like, isn't it?'

'You have a vicar coming to you?' laughed Macleod.

'I said I wanted someone to give me a boost. He'll be here soon, but I thought I owed you my thanks.'

'Very clever,' said Macleod, 'putting your hair in, but you got lucky with that. We almost didn't have any bodies to recover.'

'Seoras,' said Kirsten suddenly, 'I had to push them off the cliff. Shouldn't have to do that.' There was a quietness in her voice and she could hear Macleod thinking.

'You shouldn't have to do a lot of things,' he said. 'I shouldn't have to do things in my line of work. Anna Hunt asked me why I sent you, why I told you to go for it. I knew you'd be hurt by it. I'm hurt by what I do. It affects you, but you're good at it. You'll be one of the best. Just take care of yourself until then. Try and find the quieter pieces of the job.'

'I was two metres,' said Kirsten suddenly. 'Two metres.'

'Two metres from what?' asked Macleod.

'I'm sorry, Seoras, I can't say. I'll speak to you soon,' and rather abruptly, Kirsten switched the phone off. She bent over, hands in front of her face, and began to cry.

I was two metres from not being here, she thought to herself, *two metres from having lost it all.* Kirsten shook her head. She really had to get herself together. There was a cry from across the street. She looked up to see a hand waving at her. The owner of that hand had a smile, but she could see his concern when he saw her face. He made his way over across the road and she noticed he was in a smart suit. As he approached, she stood up, drying her eyes.

'You came,' she said.

'It's a bit of a change from the coffee shop just outside London,' he said, 'but yes, I'm here. You sounded like you needed someone.'

She reached forward and grabbed him. The man looked confused, almost overwrought, as he had the life almost squeezed out of him, Kirsten gripped him tightly. She reached up, planted a kiss on his lips, moved her hand round to the back of his neck, and stood there unashamedly in the street kissing away at him. He could hear the tears flowing as well. After a few moments, he took her hands and sat her down at the seat. Kirsten took a drink of her coffee, then took another.

'You just tell me when you're ready,' said the man. 'I'm good to talk about it with you. Anna said I can debrief you.'

'I guess she knows more than she lets on sometimes.'

'It's not about her. It's about you,' said the man.

'Two metres. I was two metres,' she said.

'Do you want to talk about it?' the man asked. 'We can go somewhere if you want.'

Kirsten looked up at him. She took a large drink of her coffee, tears still streaming down her face. Then, she stood up, walked over to him, and sat down on his lap in the seat.

'I don't want to go anywhere,' she said, 'and I don't want to talk. Just hold me.' As the man cradled Kirsten in his arms, she heard the rain as it started to pitter-patter on the man's suit and onto her hair, but Kirsten didn't care, keeping her face buried in his chest. For the next half an hour, they sat there until someone came out inquiring if the man wanted a drink. He ordered a black coffee, but when they left an hour later, it hadn't been touched. They walked along the streets of Inverness slowly making their way back towards Kirsten's home. As they did so, she felt a squeeze on her hand. She turned to the man.

He looked at her and asked, 'I take it I've made it beyond being a chauffeur then.'

Kirsten laughed. 'Well, so far, so good,' she said. 'Let's just see where this goes.'

Read on to discover the Patrick Smythe series!

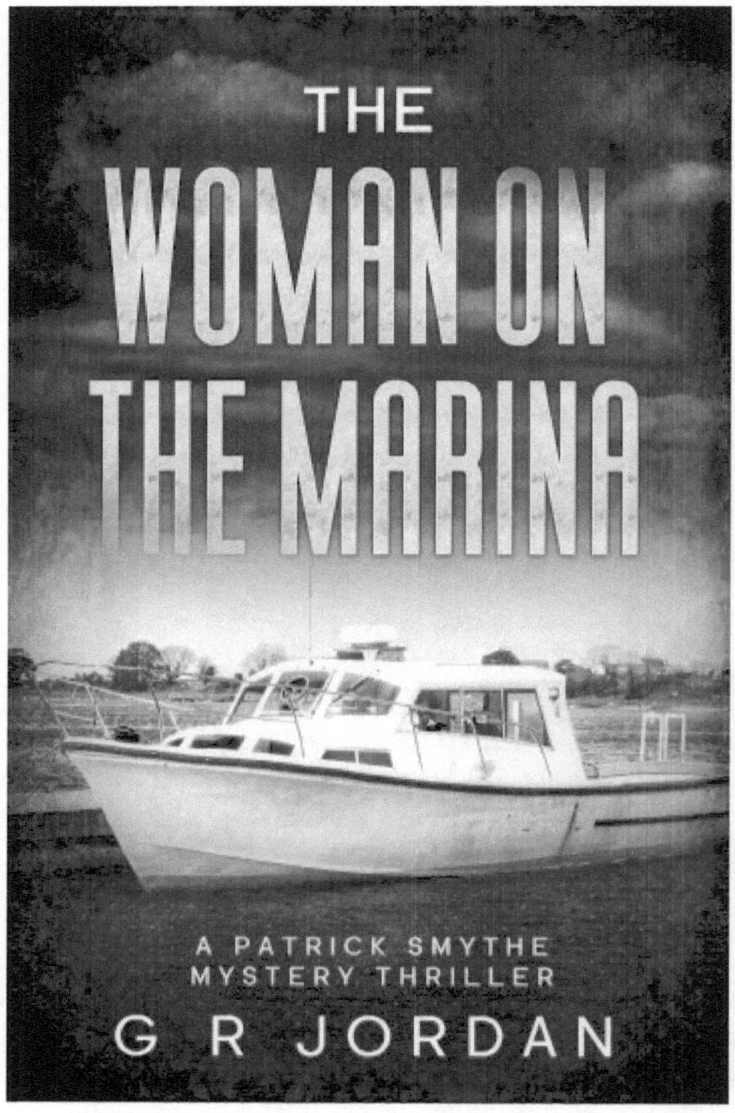

Start your Patrick Smythe journey here!

Patrick Smythe is a former Northern Irish policeman who

after suffering an amputation after a bomb blast, takes to the sea between the west coast of Scotland and his homeland to ply his trade as a private investigator. Join Paddy as he tries to work to his own ethics while knowing how to bend the rules he once enforced. Working from his beloved motorboat 'Craigantlet', Paddy decides to rescue a drug mule in this short story from the pen of G R Jordan.

Join G R Jordan's monthly newsletter about forthcoming releases and special writings for his tribe of avid readers and then receive your free Patrick Smythe short story.

Go to https://bit.ly/PatrickSmythe for your Patrick Smythe journey to start!

About the Author

GR Jordan is a self-published author who finally decided at forty that in order to have an enjoyable lifestyle, his creative beast within would have to be unleashed. His books mirror that conflict in life where acts of decency contend with self-promotion, goodness stares in horror at evil, and kindness blindsides us when we at our worst. Corrupting our world with his parade of wondrous and horrific characters, he highlights everyday tensions with fresh eyes whilst taking his methodical, intelligent mainstays on a roller-coaster ride of dilemmas, all the while suffering the banter of their provocative sidekicks.

A graduate of Loughborough University where he masqueraded as a chemical engineer but ultimately played American football, Gary had worked at changing the shape of cereal flakes and pulled a pallet truck for a living. Watching vegetables freeze at -40'C was another career highlight and he was also one of the Scottish Highlands "blind" air traffic controllers.

These days he has graduated to answering a telephone to people in trouble before telephoning other people to sort it out.

Having flirted with most places in the UK, he is now based in the Isle of Lewis in Scotland where his free time is spent between raising a young family with his wife, writing, figuring out how to work a loom and caring for a small flock of chickens. Luckily, his writing is influenced by his varied work and life experience as the chickens have not been the poetical inspiration he had hoped for!

You can connect with me on:
- https://grjordan.com
- https://facebook.com/carpetlessleprechaun

Subscribe to my newsletter:
- https://bit.ly/PatrickSmythe

Also by G R Jordan

G R Jordan writes across multiple genres including crime, dark and action adventure fantasy, feel good fantasy, mystery thriller and horror fantasy. Below is a selection of his work. Whilst all books are available across online stores, signed copies are available at his personal shop.

The Hunt for 'Red' Anna (Kirsten Stewart Thrillers #5)
https://grjordan.com/product/the-hunt-for-red-anna
London says Anna Hunt is a traitor. Kirsten is dispatched to find and eliminate her boss. Can Kirsten put aside her disbelief to complete her mission or will she find her instincts reveal even stranger truths?

When Kirsten is called to London, she finds the news of Anna Hunt's defection hard to stomach. With sketchy details, Anna's betrayal seems bizarre and the instruction to eliminate her a brutal response. On hunting down her boss, a plot with an unknown orchestrator gives doubt to every assumption. As the mystery is revealed and secrets laid bare, Kirsten finds her own team under a kill order.

You only ever know someone when you live with them!

Highlands and Islands Detective Thriller Series

https://grjordan.com/product/waters-edge

Join stalwart DI Macleod and his burgeoning new DC McGrath as they look into the darker side of the stunningly scenic and wilder parts of the north of Scotland. From the Black Isle to Lewis, from Mull to Harris and across to the small Isles, the Uists and Barra, this mismatched pairing follow murders, thieves and vengeful victims in an effort to restore tranquillity to the remoter parts of the land.

Be part of this tale of a surprise partnership amidst the foulest deeds and darkest souls who stalk this peaceful and most beautiful of lands, and you'll never see the Highlands the same way again

The Disappearance of Russell Hadleigh (Patrick Smythe Book 1)

https://grjordan.com/product/the-disappearance-of-russell-hadleigh

A retired judge fails to meet his golf partner. His wife calls for help while running a fantasy play ring. When Russians start co-opting into a fairly-traded clothing brand, can Paddy untangle the strands before the bodies start littering the golf course?

In his first full novel, Patrick Smythe, the single-armed former policeman, must infiltrate the golfing social scene to discover the fate of his client's husband. Assisted by a young starlet of the greens, Paddy tries to understand just who bears a grudge and who likes to play in the rough, culminating in a high stakes showdown where lives are hanging by the reaction of a moment. If you love pacey action, suspicious motives and devious characters, then Paddy Smythe operates amongst your kind of people.

Love is a matter of taste but money always demands more of its suitor.

Surface Tensions (Island Adventures Book 1)

https://grjordan.com/product/surface-tensions

Mermaids sighted near a Scottish island. A town exploding in anger and distrust. And Donald's got to get the sexiest fish in town, back in the water.

"Surface Tensions" is the first story in a series of Island adventures from the pen of G R Jordan. If you love comic moments, cosy adventures and light fantasy action, then you'll love these tales with a twist. Get the book that amazon readers said, "perfectly captures life in the Scottish Hebrides" and that explores "human nature at its best and worst".

Something's stirring the water!

Corpse Reviver (A Contessa Munroe Mystery #1)

https://grjordan.com/product/corspe-reviver

A widowed Contessa flees to the northern waters in search of adventure. An entrepreneur dies on an ice pack excursion. But when the victim starts moonlighting from his locked cabin, can the Contessa uncover the true mystery of his death?

Catriona Cullodena Munroe, widow of the late Count de Los Palermo, has fled the family home, avoiding the scramble for title and land. As she searches for the life she always wanted, the Contessa, in the company of the autistic and rejected Tiff, must solve the mystery of a man who just won't let his business go.

Corpse Reviver is the first murder mystery involving the formidable and sometimes downright rude lady of leisure and her straight talking niece. Bonded by blood, and thrown together by fate, join this pair of thrill seekers as they realise that flirting with danger brings a price to pay.